PRAISE FOR
KRISTINE KATHRYN RUSCH

"Rusch is a great storyteller."
—*RT Book Reviews*

"Whether [Rusch] writes high fantasy, horror, sf, or contemporary fantasy, I've always been fascinated by her ability to tell a story with that enviable gift of invisible prose. She's one of those very few writers whose style takes me right into the story—the words and pages disappear as the characters and their story swallows me whole….Rusch has style."
—Charles de Lint

"Kristine Kathryn Rusch writes stories I like to read."
—Michael Payne, *Tangent Online*

"Rusch's greatest strength…is her ability to close down a story and leave the reader feeling that the author could not possibly have wrung any more satisfaction out of the piece."
—*The Kansas City Star*

"Rusch is a great storyteller—easily the equal of Patterson or Koontz."
—*Analog*

"Kristine Kathryn Rusch is one of the best writers in the field."

—*SFRevu*

"[Rusch's] writing style is simple but elegant, and her characterization excellent."

—Mark Morris
Beyond

"Kristine Kathryn Rusch's crime stories are exceptional, both in plot and in style."

—Ed Gorman
Mystery Scene Magazines

Praise for the Retrieval Artist series

"The SF thriller is alive and well, and today's leading practitioner is Kristine Kathryn Rusch."

—*Analog*

"What links [Miles Flint] to his most memorable literary ancestors is his hard-won ability to perceive the complex nature of morality and live with the burden of his own inevitable failure."

—*Locus*

"If there's any such thing as a sci-fi CSI, the Retrieval Artist novels set the tone."

—*The Edge Boston*

PRAISE FOR THE SMOKEY DALTON SERIES
(WRITING AS KRIS NELSCOTT)

"Nelscott's series setting, in the turbulent late '60s, gives her books layers of issues of racism, class, and war, all of which still seem to remain sadly timely today."

—*Oregonian*

"Nelscott has her own, very distinct voice, and her series creates its own deeply satisfying pleasures and cogent points."

—*Seattle Times*

"Nelscott is good at conveying the edgy caution that blacks once brought to their movements among white society."

—*Houston Chronicle*

"(A) crime writer deliberately taking chances."

—*Chicago Tribune*

"It's not hard to draw parallels between Nelscott's PI Smokey Dalton and Walter Mosley's Easy Rawlins, another secretive, canny black man trying to solve mysteries while circumspectly navigating the white world. But Dalton's no knock-off. (Would you label the hundreds of hard-boiled detectives who've appeared in Raymond Chandler's wake mere Marlow Xeroxes because they're white?)"

—*Entertainment Weekly*

Also by
Kristine Kathryn Rusch

The Retrieval Artist Series:

The Disappeared
Extremes
Consequences
Buried Deep
Paloma
Recovery Man
Duplicate Effort
Anniversary Day
Blowback

The Smokey Dalton Series (as Kris Nelscott):

A Dangerous Road
Smoke-Filled Rooms
Thin Walls
Stone Cribs
War at Home
Days of Rage
Street Justice (March 2014)

Five California Tales
Kristine Kathryn Rusch

*wmg*PUBLISHING

Five California Tales

Copyright © 2013 by Kristine Kathryn Rusch
Published 2013 by WMG Publishing
www.wmgpublishing.com
Cover art copyright © Mypix/Dreamstime
Book and cover design copyright © 2013 by WMG Publishing
Cover design by Allyson Longueira/WMG Publishing
ISBN-13: 978-0-615-85790-9
ISBN-10: 0-615-85790-6

"Spirit Guides" by Kristine Kathryn Rusch was first published in *Heaven Sent,* edited by Peter Crowther, Daw Books, 1995.

"The Perfect Man" by Kristine Kathryn Rusch was first published in *Murder Most Romantic,* edited by Martin H. Greenberg and Denise Little, Cumberland House Press, 2001.

"Ghosts" by Kristine Kathryn Rusch was first published in *Death By Horoscope,* edited by Anne Perry, Carroll and Graf, August 2001.

"Stomping Mad" by Kristine Kathryn Rusch was first published in *Return of the Dinosaurs,* edited by Mike Resnick and Martin H. Greenberg, Daw Books, 1997.

"Monuments to the Dead" by Kristine Kathryn Rusch was first appeared in *Tales From the Great Turtle,* edited by Piers Anthony, Richard Gilliam, and Martin H. Greenberg, Tor Books, December 1994.

Contents

Five California Tales
Kristine Kathryn Rusch

Introduction

I WRITE A LOT ABOUT CALIFORNIA, even though I've never lived in the state. Some of the inspiration for what I write comes from proximity: those of us who live in Oregon hear about California all the time. Sometimes it's from the California tourists. Sometimes it's the local news. And sometimes it's from folks who live outside the Pacific Northwest who seem to think the only state on the West Coast is California.

Then there's the Oregon reaction to California, which was once the not-so-unofficial state slogan: *Please Don't Californicate Oregon.* And then there's the Oregon curse, made popular in the movie *Die Hard* (and, oddly enough, spoken by a New Yorker): *Cali-fuckin-fornia.*

You'd think we hate California here. But we don't. Or at least, I don't. There's so much history in our neighbor to the south, so much wealth, and so much craziness. Whatever Oregon has, California has it times ten. Plus the state has different environments. Northern California has more ties to Oregon than it does to Southern

California, which has a lot more in common with the rest of the Southwest.

I've written about all of it—or almost all of it. (I don't think I've written much about the mountains yet.) In this volume, you'll find five stories of different genres and different moods. The only things they have in common are the author and an important California tie.

"Spirit Guides" starts in Los Angeles. In fact, when I think of the story, I think of it as a particularly LA kinda story, even though it has other settings. I would call "Spirit Guides" a dark fantasy but I think it's an early example of a more modern genre, fantasy noir.

Then there's "The Perfect Man." This story also has a detective and a California setting, but there the similarity ends. Because this is a romantic suspense tale with a touch of satire. And this one is set in San Francisco.

"Ghosts" is another noir tale that, despite its title, belongs to the mystery genre. Like "Spirit Guides," "Ghosts" features a character who travels, but he travels through California on an important part of his trip.

"Stomping Mad" takes place at a science fiction convention in California. Like "Ghosts," "Stomping Mad" feels cross-genre, although it isn't. "Stomping Mad" marks the first appearance of my popular series character Spade, who solves crimes at sf cons.

And finally, a slipstream story that might be fantasy and might not. "Monuments To The Dead" takes place at Mount Rushmore, but the journalist in the story is writing an article for a California magazine, sharing the

California perspective. California colors her attitudes and the story itself.

I'm constantly surprised at how much California figures into my fiction. There will be other California short story volumes in the future as I continue to review my backlist for WMG Publishing. In the meantime, enjoy this one.

—Kristine Kathryn Rusch
Lincoln City, Oregon
November 11, 2011

Spirit Guides

*L*OS ANGELES. City of the Angels.

Kincaid walked down Hollywood Boulevard, his feet stepping on gum-coated stars. Cars whooshed past him, horns honking, tourists gawking. The line outside Graumann's Chinese clutched purses against their sides, held windbreakers tightly over their arms. A hooker leaned against the barred display window of the corner drugstore, her make-up so thick it looked like a mask in the hot sun.

The shooting had left him shaken. The crazy had opened up inside a nearby Burger Joint, slaughtering four customers and three teenaged kids behind the counter before three men, passing on the street, rushed inside and grabbed him. Half a dozen shots had gone wild, leaving fist-sized holes in the drywall, shattering picture frames, and making one perfect circle in the center of the cardboard model for a bacon-double cheeseburger.

He'd arrived two minutes too late, hearing the call on his police scanner on his way home, but unable to maneuver in traffic. Christ, some of those people who wouldn't let him pass might have had relatives in that Burger Joint. Still and all, he had arrived first to find the killer trussed up in a chair, the men hovering around him, women clutching sobbing children, blood and bodies mixing with French fries on the unswept floor.

A little girl, no more than three, had grabbed his sleeve and pointed at one of the bodies, long slender male and young, wearing a '49ers t-shirt, ripped jeans and Nikes, face a bloody mass of tissue, and said, "Make him better," in a whisper that broke Kincaid's heart. He cuffed the suspect, roped off the area, took names of witnesses before the backup arrived. Three squads, fresh-faced uniformed officers, followed by the swat team, nearly five minutes too late, the forensic team and the ambulances not far behind.

Kincaid had lit a cigarette with shaking fingers and said, "All yours," before taking off into the sun-drenched crowded streets.

He stopped outside the Roosevelt, and peered into the plate glass. His own tennis shoes were stained red, and a long brown streak of drying blood marked his Levi's. The cigarette had burned to a coal between his nicotine-stained fingers, and he tossed it, stamping it out on the star of a celebrity whose name he didn't recognize.

Inside stood potted palms and faded glamour. Pictures of motion picture stars long dead lined the second floor balcony. Within the last ten years, the hotel's management had restored the Roosevelt to its 1920s glory, when it had been the site for the first-ever Academy Award celebration. When he first came to L.A., he spent a lot of time in the hotel, imagining the low-cut dresses, the clink of champagne flutes, the scattered applause as the nominees were announced. Searching for a kind of beauty that existed only in celluloid, a product of light and shadows and nothing more.

El Pueblo de Nuestra Señora la Reina de los Angeles de Porciuncula.

The City of Our Lady, Queen of the Angels of Porciuncula.

He knew nothing of the Angels of Porciuncula, did not know why Filipe de Neve in 1781 named the city after them. He suspected it was some kind of prophecy, but he didn't know.

They had been fallen angels.

Of that he was sure.

He sighed, wiped the sweat from his forehead with a grimy hand, then returned to his car, knowing that home and sleep would elude him for one more night.

***

LEAN AND SPARE, Kincaid survived on cigarettes, coffee, chocolate and bourbon. Sometime in the last five years, he had allowed the LAPD to hire him, although he had no formal training. After a few odd run-ins and one overnight jail stay before it became clear that Kincaid wasn't anywhere near the crime scene, Kincaid had met Davis, his boss. Davis had the flat gaze of a man who had seen too much, and he knew, from the records and the evidence before him, that Kincaid was too precious to lose. He made Kincaid a plainclothes detective and never assigned him a partner.

Kincaid never told anyone what he did. Most of the cops he worked with never knew. All they cared about was that when Kincaid was on the job, suspects were found, cases were closed, and files were sealed. He worked quietly and he got results.

They didn't need him on this one. The perp was caught at the scene. All Kincaid had to do was write his report, then go home, toss the sneakers in the trash, soak the Levi's, and wait for another day.

But it wasn't that easy. He sat in his car, an olive Green 1968 Olds with a fading pine-shaped air freshener hanging from the rearview mirror, long after his colleagues had left. His hands were still shaking, his nostrils still coated with the scent of blood and burgers, his ears clogged with the faint sobs of a pimply faced boy rocking over the body of a fallen co-worker. The images would stick, along with all of the others. His brain was reaching overload. Had been for a long time. But that little girl's voice, the plea in her tone, had been more than he could bear.

For twenty years, he had tried to escape, always ending up in a new town, with new problems. Shootings in Oklahoma parking lots, bombings in upstate New York, murders in restaurants and shopping malls and suburban family pickups. The violence surrounded him, and he was trapped.

Surely this time, they would let him get away.

A hooker knocked on the window of his car. He thought he could smell the sweat and perfume through the rolled-up glass. Her cleavage was mottled, her cheap elastic top revealing the top edge of brown nipple.

He shook his head, then turned the ignition and grabbed the gear shift on the column to take the car out of park. The Olds roared to life, and with it came the adrenalin rush, hormones tinged with panic. He pulled out of the parking space, past the hooker, down Hollywood Boulevard toward the first freeway intersection he could find.

Kincaid would disappear from the LAPD as mysteriously as he had arrived. He stopped long enough to pick up his clothes, his credit cards, and a hand-painted coffee mug a teenaged girl in Galveston had given him twenty years before, when she mistakenly thought he had saved her life.

He merged into the continuous LA rush hour traffic for the last time, radio off, clutching the wheel in white-knuckled tightness. He would go to Big Bear, up in the mountains, where there were no people, no crimes, nothing except himself and the wilderness.

He drove away from the angels.

Or so he hoped.

***

KINCAID DROVE until he realized he was on the road to Las Vegas. He pulled the Olds over, put on his hazards and bowed his head, unwilling to go any farther. But he knew, even if he didn't drive there, he would wake up in Vegas, his car in the lot outside. It had happened before.

He didn't remember taking the wrong turn, but he wasn't supposed to remember. They were just telling him that his work wasn't done, the work they had forced him to do ever since he was a young boy.

With a quick, vicious movement, he got out of the Olds and shook his fist at the star-filled desert sky. "I can't take it any more, do you hear me?"

But no shape flew across the moon, no angel wings brushed his cheek, no reply filled his heart. He could turn around, but the roads he drove would only lead him back to Los Angeles, back to people, back to murders in which little girls stood in pools of blood. He knew what Los Angeles was like. Maybe they would allow him a few days rest in Vegas.

Las Vegas, the fertile plains, originally founded in the late 1700s like L.A., only the settlement didn't become permanent until 1905 when the first lots were sold (and nearly flooded out 5 years later). He thought maybe the city's youth and brashness would be a tonic, but even as he drove into town, he felt the blood beneath the surface. Despair and hopelessness had come to every place in America. Only here it mingled with the cajing-jing of slot machines and the smell of money.

He wanted to stay in the MGM Grand, but the Olds wouldn't drive through the lot. He settled on a cheap tumble-down hotel on the far side of the strip, complete with chenille bedspreads and rattling window air conditioners that dripped water on the thin brown indoor-outdoor carpet. There he slept in the protective dark of the black-out curtains, and dreamed:

Angels floated above him, wings so long the tips brushed his face. As he watched, they tucked their wings around themselves and plummeted, eagle-like, to the ground below, banking when the concrete of a major superhighway rose in front of them. He was on the bed, watching, helpless, knowing that each time the long white tail feathers touched the earth, violence erupted somewhere it had never been before.

He started awake, coughing the deep racking cough of a three-pack-a-day man. His tongue was thick and tasted of bad coffee and nicotine. He reached for the end table, clicking on the brown glass bubble lamp, then grabbed his lighter and a cigarette from the pack resting on top of the cut-glass ashtray. His hands were still shaking, and the room was quiet except for his labored breathing. Only in the silence did he realize that his dream had been accompanied by the sound of the pimply faced boy, sobbing.

***

IT HAPPENED JUST BEFORE DAWN. A woman's scream, outside, cut off in mid-thrum, followed by a sickening thud and footsteps. He had known it would, the minute the car had refused to enter the Grand's parking lot. And he had to respond, whether it was his choice or not.

Kincaid paused long enough to pull on his pants, checking to make sure his wallet was in the back pocket. Then he grabbed his key and let himself out of the room.

His window overlooked the pool, a liver-shaped thing built in the late fifties of blue tile. The management left the terrace lights on all night, and Kincaid used those to guide him across the interior courtyard. In the half-light, he saw another shape running toward the pool, a pear-shaped man dressed in the too-tight uniform of a national rent-a-cop service. The air smelled of chlorine and the desert heat was still heavy despite the early morning hour. Leaves and dead bugs floated in the water, and the surrounding patio furniture was so dirty it took a moment for Kincaid to realize it was supposed to be white.

The rent-a-cop had already arrived on the scene, his pasty skin turning green as he looked down. Kincaid came up behind him, stopped, and stared.

The body was crumpled behind the removable diving board. One look at her blood-stained face, swollen and bruised neck, her chipped and broken fingernails and he knew.

All of it.

"I'd better call this in," the rent-a-cop said, and Kincaid shook his head, knowing that if he were alone with the body, he would end up spending the next few days in a Las Vegas lock-up.

"No, let me." He went back to his room, packed his meager possessions and set them by the door. Then he called 911 and reported the murder, slipping on a shirt before going back outside.

The rent-a-cop was wiping his mouth with the back of his hand. The air smelled of vomit. Kincaid said nothing. Together they waited for the Nevada authorities to show: a skinny plainclothes detective whose eyes were red-rimmed from lack of sleep and his female partner, busty and official in regulation blue.

While the partner radioed in, the rent-a-cop told his version: that he had been making his rounds and heard a couple arguing poolside. He was watching from the window when the man back-handed the woman, and then took off through the casino. The woman didn't get up, and the cop decided to check on her instead of chasing the guy. Kincaid had shown up a minute or two later from his room in the hotel.

The plainclothes man turned his flat gaze on Kincaid. Kincaid flashed his LAPD badge, then told the plainclothes man that the killer's name was Luther Hardy, that he'd killed her because her anger was the last straw in a day that had seen him lose most of their $10,000 savings on the Mirage's roulette table. Even as the men spoke, Hardy was sitting at the only open craps table in Circus Circus, betting $25 chips on the come line.

Then Kincaid waited for the disbelief, but the plainclothesman nodded, thanked him, rounded up the female partner and headed toward Circus Circus, leaving Kincaid, not the rent-a-cop, to guard the scene. Kincaid rubbed his nose with his thumb and forefinger, trying to stop a building headache, feeling the rent-a-cop's scrutiny. Kincaid could always pick them, the ones who had seen everything, the ones who had learned through hard experience and crazy knocks to check any lead that came their way. Like Davis. Only Kincaid was new to this plainclothesman, so there would be a hundred questions when they returned.

Questions Kincaid was too tired to answer.

He told the rent-a-cop his room number, then staggered back, picked up his things and checked out, figuring he would be halfway to Phoenix before they discovered he was gone for good. They would call LAPD, and Davis would realize that Kincaid had finally left, and would probably light a candle for him later that evening because he would know that Kincaid's singular talent was still controlling his life.

***

LIKE A HICK TOURIST, Kincaid stopped on the Hoover Dam. At eight a.m., he stood on the miraculous concrete structure, staring at the raging blue of the Colorado below. An angel fluttered past him, then wrapped its wings around its torso and dove like a gull after prey. It disappeared in the glare of the sunlight against the water, and he strained, hoping and fearing he'd catch a glimpse as the angel rose, dripping, from the water.

The glimpses had haunted him since he was thirteen. He'd been in St. Patrick's Cathedral with his mother, and one of the stained glass angels left her window, floated through the air, and kissed him before alighting on the pulpit to tickle the visiting priest during Mass. The priest hadn't noticed the feathers brush his face and neck, but he had died the next day in a mugging outside the sub-way station at 63rd and Lexington.

Kincaid hadn't seen the mugging, but his train had arrived only a few seconds after the priest died.

Years later, Kincaid finally thought to wonder why he hadn't died from the angel's kiss. And, although he still didn't have the answer, he knew that his second sight came from that morning. All he needed to do was look at a body to know who had driven the spirit from it, and why. The snapshots remained in his mind in all their horror, surrounded by faces frozen in agony, each shot a sharp moment of pain that pierced a hole in his increasingly fragile soul.

As a young man, he believed he could stop the pain, that he had been given the gift so that he could end the horrors. He would ride out, like St. George, and defeat the dragon that had terrified the village. But these terrors were as old as time itself, and instead of stopping them, Kincaid could only observe them, and report what his inner eye had seen. He had thought, as he grew older, that using his skills to imprison the perpetrators would help, but the deaths continued, more each year, and the little girl in the Burger Joint had provided the final straw.

Make him better.

Kincaid didn't have that kind of magic.

The angel flew out of the wide crevice, past the canyon walls, its tail feathers dripping just as Kincaid had feared. Somewhere within a two-hundred-mile radius, someone would die violently because an angel had brushed the earth. Kincaid hunched himself against the bright morning, then turned and walked along the rock-strewn highway to his car. When he got inside, he kept the radio off so that the news of the atrocity would not hit him when it happened.

But the silence wouldn't keep him ignorant forever. He would turn on the TV in a hotel, or pass a row of newspapers outside a restaurant, and the information would present itself to him, as clearly and brightly as it always had, as if it were his responsibility, subject to his control.

***

THE CAR LED HIM INTO PHOENIX. From the freeway, the city was a row of concrete lanes, marred by machine painted lines. From the side streets, it had well manicured lawns and tidy houses, too many strip restaurants and the ubiquitous mall. He was having a chimichanga in a neighborhood Garcia's when he watched the local news and realized that he might not hear of an atrocity after all. He finished the meal and left before the national news aired.

He was still in Phoenix at midnight, and had not yet found a hotel. He didn't want to sleep, didn't want to be led to the next place where someone would die. He was sitting alone at a small table in a high-class strip joint, sipping bourbon that actually had a smooth bite instead of the cheap stuff he normally got. The strippers were legion, all young, with tits high and firm and asses to match. Some had long lean legs and others were all torso. But none approached him, as if a sign were flashing above him, warning the women away. He drank until he could feel it—he didn't know how many drinks that was any more—and was startled that no one noticed him getting tight.

Even drunk, he couldn't relax, couldn't laugh. Enjoyment had leached out of him, decades ago.

When the angel appeared in front of him, he thought it was another stripper, taller than most, wrapped in gossamer wings. Then it unfolded the wings and extended them, gently, as if it were doing a slow-motion fan dance, and he realized that its face had no features, and its body was fat and nippleless like a butterfly.

He raised his glass to it. "You gonna kiss me again?" His thoughts had seemed clear, but the words came out slurred.

The angel said nothing—it probably couldn't speak since it had no mouth. It merely took the drink from him, and set the glass on the table. Then it grabbed his hand, pulled him to his feet, and led him from the room like a recalcitrant child. He vaguely wondered how he looked, stumbling alone through the maze of people, his right arm outstretched.

When the fresh air hit him, the bourbon backed up in his throat like bile. He staggered away from the beefy valets behind the potted cactus, and threw up, the angel standing beside him, still as a statue. After a moment, he stood up and wiped his mouth with the crumpled hand-kerchief he kept folded in his back pocket. He still felt drunk, but not as bloated.

Then the angel scooped him in its arms. Its body was soft and cold as if it contained no life at all. It cradled him like a baby, and they flew up until the city became a blaze of lights.

The wind ruffled his hair and woke him even more. He felt strangely calm, and he attributed that to the alco-hol. Just as he was getting used to the oddness, the angel wrapped its wings around them and plummeted toward the ground.

They were moving so fast, he could feel the force of the air like a slap in his face. He was screaming—he could feel it, ripping at his throat—but he could hear nothing. They hurtled over the interstate. The cars were the size of ants before the angel extended its wings to ease their landing.

The angel tilted them upright, and they touched down in an empty glass strewn parking lot that led to an insurance office whose door was surrounded by yellow police tape. He recognized the site from the local newscast he had caught in Garcia's: ever since eight that morning, the insurance office had been the location of a hostage situation. A husband had decided to terror-ize his wife who worked inside and, although shots had been fired, no one had been injured.

He stared at the building, felt the terror radiate from its walls as if it were a furnace. The insurance company was an old one: the gold lettering on the hand-painted window was chipped, and inside, he could barely make out the shape of an overturned chair. He turned to ask the angel why it had brought him there, when he realized it was gone.

Kincaid stood in the parking lot for a moment, one hand wrapped around his stomach, the other holding his throbbing head. They had flown for miles. He still had his wallet, but had no idea where he was or how he would find a pay phone.

And he didn't know what the angel had wanted from him.

He sighed and walked across the parking lot. The broken glass crunched beneath his shoes. His mouth was dry. The police tape looked too yellow in the glare of the streetlight. He stood on the stoop and peered inside, half hearing the voices from earlier in the day, the shouts from the police bullhorn, the low tense voice of the wife, the terse clipped tones of her husband. About noon he had gone outside to smoke a cigarette—his wife hated smoke—and had shot a stray dog to ward off the policeman who had been sneaking up behind him.

Kincaid could smell the death. He followed his nose to the side of the building. There, among the gravel and the spindly flowerless rose bushes, lay the dog on its side. It was scrawny and its coat was mottled. Its tongue protruded just a bit from its open mouth. Its glassy eyes seemed to follow Kincaid, and he wondered how the news had missed this, the sympathy story amidst all the horror.

The stations in LA would have covered it.

Poor dog. A stray in life, unremembered in death. Just standing over it, he could see the last moments—the enticing smell of food from the police cars suddenly mingled with the scent of human fear, the glittery eyes of the male human and then pain, sharp, deep, and complete.

Kincaid crouched beside it. In all his years, he had never touched a dead thing, never felt the cold lifeless body, never totally understood how a body could live and then not live within the same instant. In the past he had left the dead for someone else to clean up, but here no one would. The dog would rot in this site of trauma and near-human tragedy, and no one would take the care to bury the dead.

Perhaps that was why the angel brought him, to show him that there had been carnage after all.

He didn't know how to bury it. All he had were his hands. But he touched the soft soil of the rose garden, his wrist brushing the dog's tail as he did so.

The dog coughed and struggled to sit up.

Kincaid backed away so quickly he nearly fell. The dog choked, then coughed again, spraying blood all over the bushes, the gravel, and the concrete. It looked at him with a mixture of fear and pain.

"Jesus," Kincaid muttered.

He pushed himself forward, then grabbed the dog's shoulders. Its labored breathing eased and its tail thumped slightly against the ground. Something clattered against the pavement, and he saw the bullet, rolling away. The dog stood, whimpered, licked his hand, and then trotted off to fill its empty stomach.

Kincaid sat down in the glass and gravel, staring at his blood-covered hands.

Phoenix.

A creature of myth that rose from its own ashes to live again.

He had been such a fool.

All those years. All those lives.

Such a fool.

He looked up at the star-filled desert sky. The angel that had brought him hovered over him like a teacher waiting to see if the student understood the lecture. He couldn't relive his life, but maybe, just maybe, he could help one little girl who had spoken with the voice of angels.

Make him better.

"Take me to back to Los Angeles," he said to the angel. "To the people who died yesterday."

***

AND IN A HEARTBEAT, he was back in the Burger Joint. The killer, an overweight acne-scarred man with empty eyes, was tied to a chair near the window, a group of men milling nervously around him, the gun leaning against the wall behind them. All the children were crying, their parents pressing the tiny faces against shoulders, trying to block the sight. The air smelled of burgers and fresh blood.

A little girl, no more than three, grabbed Kincaid's sleeve and pointed at one of the bodies, long slender male and young, wearing a '49ers t-shirt, ripped jeans and Nikes, face a bloody mass of tissue, and said, "Make him better," in a whisper that broke Kincaid's heart.

Kincaid crouched, hands shaking, wishing desperately for a cigarette, and grabbed the body by the arm. Air whistled from the lungs, and the blood bubbled in the remains of the face. As Kincaid watched, the face returned, the blood disappeared and a young man was staring at him with fear-filled eyes.

"You all right, friend?" Kincaid asked.

The man nodded and the little girl flung herself in his arms.

"Jesus," someone said behind him.

Kincaid shook his head. "It's amazing how bad injuries can look when someone's covered with blood."

He didn't wait for the response, just went to the next body and the next, his need for a cigarette decreasing with touch, the blood drying as if it had never been. When he got behind the counter, he gently pushed aside the pimply faced boy sobbing over the dead co-worker, and then he paused.

If he reversed this one, they would have nothing to indict the killer on.

The boy's breath hitched as he watched Kincaid. Kincaid turned and looked over his shoulder at the killer tied to the chair near the entrance. Holes the size of fists marred the drywall and made one perfect circle in the center of the cardboard model for a bacon-double cheeseburger. It would be enough.

He grabbed the body's shoulders, feeling the grease of the uniform beneath his fingers. The spirit slid back in as if it had never left, and the wounds sealed themselves as they would on a video tape run backwards.

All those years. All those wasted years.

"How did you do that?" the pimply faced boy asked, his face shiny with tears.

"He was only stunned," Kincaid said.

When he was done, he went outside to find the backup team interviewing witnesses, the ambulances just arriving, five minutes too late.

"All yours," he said, before taking off into the sun-drenched crowded streets.

Now he had to keep moving. No jobs with police departments, no comfortable apartments. He had to stay one step ahead of a victim's shock, one step ahead of the press who would someday catch wind of his ability. He couldn't let them corner him, because the power was not his to control.

He was still trapped.

He stopped outside the Roosevelt, lit a cigarette, and peered into the plate glass. His own tennis shoes were stained red, and a long brown streak of drying blood marked his Levi's. The cigarette had burned to a coal between his nicotine stained fingers before he had a chance to take a drag, and he tossed it, stamping it out on the star of a celebrity whose name he didn't recognize.

All those years and he never knew. The kiss made some kind of cosmic sense. Even Satan, the head of the fallen angels, was once beloved of God. Even Satan must have felt remorse at the pain he caused. He would never be accepted back into the fold, but he might use his powers to repair some of the pain he caused. Only he wouldn't be able to alone, for each time he touched the earth, he would cause another death. What better to do, then, but to give healing power to a child, who would learn and grow into the role.

Kincaid's hands were still shaking. The blood had crusted beneath his fingernails.

"I never asked for this!" he shouted, and people didn't even turn as they passed on the street. Shouting crazies were common in Hollywood. He held his hands to the sky. "I never asked for this!"

Above him, angels flew like eagles, soaring and dipping and diving, never coming close enough to endanger the Earth. Their featureless faces radiated a kind of joy. And, although he would never admit it, he felt that joy too.

Although he would not slay the dragon, he wouldn't have to live with its carnage either. Finally, at last, he could make some kind of difference. He let his hands fall to his side, and wondered if the Roosevelt would shirk at letting him wash the blood off inside. He was about to ask when a stray dog pushed its muzzle against his thigh.

"Ah, hell," he said, looking down and recognizing the mottled fur, the wary yet trusting eyes. He glanced up, saw one angel hovering. A gift then, for finally understanding. He touched the dog on the back of its neck, and led it to the Olds. The dog jumped inside as if it knew the car. Kincaid sat for a moment, resting his shaking hands against the steering column.

A hooker knocked on the window. He thought he could smell the sweat and perfume through the rolled up glass. Her cleavage was mottled, her cheap elastic top revealing the top edge of brown nipple.

He shook his head, then turned the ignition and grabbed the gearshift on the column to take the car out of park. The dog barked once, and he grinned at it, before driving home to get his things. This time he wouldn't try Big Bear. This time he would go wherever the spirit led him.

The Perfect Man

*P*AIGE RACETTE STARED AT HERSELF in the full-length mirror, hands on hips. Golden cap of blond hair expertly curled, narrow chin, high cheekbones, china blue eyes, and a little too much of a figure—thanks to the fact she spent most of her day on her butt and sometimes (usually!) forgetting to exercise. The black cocktail dress with its swirling party skirt hid most of the excess, and the glittering beads around the collar brought attention to her face, always and forever her best asset.

Even with the extra pounds, she was not blind date material. Never had been. Until she quit her day job at the television station, she'd had to turn men away. Ironic that once she became a best-selling romance writer, she couldn't get a date to save her life. Part of the problem was that after she quit, she moved to San Francisco where she'd always wanted to live. She bought a Queen Anne in an old, exclusive neighborhood, set up her office in the bay windows of the second floor, and decided she was in heaven.

Little did she realize that working at home would isolate her, and being in a new city would isolate her more. It had taken her a year to make friends—mostly women, whom she met at the gym not too far from her home.

She saw interesting men, but didn't speak to them. She was still a small town girl at heart, one who was afraid of the kind of men who lurked in the big city, who believed that the only way to meet the right man was after getting to know him through mutual interests—or mutual friends.

In fact, she wouldn't have agreed to this blind date if a friend hadn't convinced her. Sally Myer was her racquetball partner and general confidant who seemed to know everyone in this city. She'd finally tired of Paige's complaining and set her up.

Paige slid on her high heels. Who'd ever thought she'd get this desperate? And then she sighed. She wasn't desperate. She was lonely.

And surely, there was no shame in that.

***

SALLY HAD PICKED the time and location, and had told Paige to dress up. Sally wasn't going to introduce them. She felt that would be tacky and make the first meeting uncomfortable. She asked Paige for a photograph to give to the blind date—one Josiah Wells—and then told Paige that he would find her.

The location was an upscale restaurant near the Opera House. It was The Place To Go at the moment—famous chef, famous food, and one of those bars that looked like it had come out of a movie set—large and open where Anyone Who Was Someone could see and be seen.

Paige arrived five minutes early, habitually prompt even when she didn't want to be. She adjusted the white pashmina shawl she'd wrapped around her bare shoulders and scanned the bar before she went in.

It was all black and chrome, with black tinted mirrors and huge black vases filled with calla lilies separating the booths. The bar itself was black marble and behind it, bottles of liquor pressed against an untinted mirror, making the place look even bigger than it was.

She had only been here once before, with her Hollywood agent and a movie producer who was interested in her second novel. He didn't buy it—the rights went to another studio for high six figures—but he had bought her some of her most memorable meals in the City by the Bay.

She sat at the bar and ordered a Chardonnay which she didn't plan on touching—she wanted to keep her wits about her this night. Even with Sally's recommendation, Paige didn't trust a man she had never met before. She'd heard too many bad stories.

Of course, all the ones she'd written were about people who saw each other across a crowded room and knew at once that they were soul mates. She had never experienced love at first sight (and sometimes she joked to her editor that it was lust at first sight) but she was still hopeful enough to believe in it.

She took the cool glass of Chardonnay that the bartender handed her and swiveled slightly in her chair so that she would be in profile, not looking anxious, but visible enough to be recognizable. And as she did, she saw a man enter the bar.

He was tall and broad-shouldered, wearing a perfectly tailored black suit that shimmered like silk. He wore a white scarf around his neck—which on him looked like the perfect fashion accent—and a red rose in his lapel. His dark hair was expertly styled away from his chiseled features, and she felt her breath catch.

Lust at first sight. It was all she could do to keep from grinning at herself.

He appeared to be looking for someone. Finally, his gaze settled on her, and he smiled.

Something about that smile didn't quite fit on his face. It was too personal. And then she shook the feeling away. She didn't want to be on a blind date—that was all. She had been fantasizing, the way she did when she was thinking of her books, and she was simply caught off guard. No man was as perfect as her heroes. No man could be, not and still be human.

Although this man looked perfect. His rugged features were exactly like ones she had described in her novels.

He crossed the room, the smile remaining, hand extended. "Paige Racette? I'm Josiah Wells."

His voice was high and a bit nasal. She took his hand, and found the palm warm and moist.

"Nice to meet you," she said, removing her hand as quickly as possible.

He wore tinted blue contacts, and the swirling lenses made his eyes seem shiny, a little too intense. In fact, everything about him was a little too intense. He leaned too close, and he seemed too eager. Perhaps he was just as nervous as she was.

"I have reservations here if you don't mind," he said.

"No, that's fine."

He extended his arm—the perfect gentleman—and she took the elbow in her hand, trying to remember the last time a man had done that for her. Her father maybe, when they went to the father-daughter dinner at her church back when she was in high school. And not one man since.

Although all the men in her books did it. When she wrote about it, the gesture seemed to have an old-fashioned elegance. In real life, it made her feel awkward.

He led her through the bar, placing one hand possessively over hers. This exact scene had happened in her first novel, *Beneath a Lover's Moon*. Fabian Garret and Skye Michaels had met, exchanged a few words, and were suddenly walking together like lovers. And Skye had thrilled to Fabian's touch.

Paige wished Josiah Wells's fingers weren't so clammy.

He led them to the maitre d', gave his name, and let the maitre d' lead them to a table near the back. See and Be Seen. Apparently they weren't important enough.

"I asked for a little privacy," he said, as if reading her thoughts. "I hope you don't mind."

She didn't. She had never liked the display aspect of this restaurant anyway.

The table was in a secluded corner. Two candles burned on silver candlesticks and the table was strewn with miniature carnations. A magnum of champagne cooled in a silver bucket, and she didn't have to look at the label to know that it was Dom Perignon.

The hair on the back of her neck rose. This was just like another scene in *Beneath a Lover's Moon*.

Josiah smiled down at her and she made herself smile at him. Maybe he thought her books were a blueprint to romancing her. She would have said so not five minutes before.

He pulled out her chair, and she sat, letting her shawl drape around her. As Josiah sat across from her, the maitre d' handed her the leather bound menu and she was startled to realize it had no prices on it. A lady's menu. She hadn't seen one of those in years. The last time she had eaten here had been lunch, not dinner, and she had remembered the prices on the menu from that meal. They had nearly made her choke on her water.

A waiter poured the champagne and left discretely, just like the maitre d' did. Josiah was watching her, his gaze intense.

She knew she had to say something. She was going to say how nice this was but she couldn't get the lie through her lips. Instead she said as warmly as she could, "You've read my books."

If anything, his gaze brightened. "I adore your books."

She made herself smile. She had been hoping he would say no, that Sally had been helping him all along. Instead, the look in his eyes made her want to push her chair even farther from the table. She had seen that look a hundred times at book signings: the too-eager fan who would easily monopolize all of her time at the expense of everyone else in line; the person who believed that his connection with the author—someone he hadn't met—was so personal that she felt the connection too.

"I didn't realize that Sally told you I wrote."

"She didn't have to. When I found out that she knew you, I asked her for an introduction."

An introduction at a party would have done nicely, where Paige could smile at him, listen for a polite moment, and then ease away. But Sally hadn't known Paige that long, and didn't understand the difficulties a writer sometimes faced. Writers rarely got recognized in person—it wasn't their faces that were famous after all but their names—but when it happened, it could become as unpleasant as it was for athletes or movie stars.

"She didn't tell me you were familiar with my work," Paige said, ducking her head behind the menu.

"I asked her not to. I wanted this to be a surprise." He was leaning forward, his manicured hand outstretched.

She looked at his fingers, curled against the linen tablecloth, carefully avoiding the miniature carnations, and wondered if his skin was still clammy.

"Since you know what I do," she continued in that too-polite voice she couldn't seem to shake, "why don't you tell me about yourself?"

"Oh," he said, "there isn't much to tell."

And then he proceeded to describe his work with a software company. She only half listened, staring at the menu, wondering if there was an easy—and polite—way to leave this meal, knowing there was not. She would make the best of it, and call Sally the next morning, warning her not to do this ever again.

"Your books," he was saying, "made me realize that women looked at men the way that men looked at women. I started to exercise and dress appropriately and I…"

She looked over the menu at him, noting the suit again. It must have been silk, and he wore it the way her heroes wore theirs. Right down to the scarf, and the rose in the lapel. The red rose, a symbol of true love from her third novel, *Without Your Love.*

That shiver ran through her again.

This time he noticed. "Are you all right?"

"Fine," she lied. "I'm just fine."

***

SOMEHOW SHE MADE IT through the meal, feeling her skin crawl as he used phrases from her books, imitated the gestures of her heroes, and presumed an intimacy with her that he didn't have. She tried to keep the conversation light and impersonal, but it was a battle that she really didn't win.

Just before the dessert course, she excused herself and went to the ladies room. After she came out, she asked the maitre d' to call her a cab, and then to signal her when it arrived. He smiled knowingly. Apparently he had seen dates end like this all too often.

She took her leave from Josiah just after they finished their coffees, thanking him profusely for a memorable evening. And then she escaped into the night, thankful that she had been careful when making plans. He didn't have her phone number and address. As she slipped into the cracked backseat of the cab, she promised herself that on the next blind date—if there was another blind date—she would make it drinks only. Not dinner. Never again.

✦✦✦

THE NEXT DAY, she and Sally met for lattes at an overpriced touristy café on the Wharf. It was their usual spot—a place where they could watch crowds and not be overheard when they decided to gossip.

"How did you meet him?" Paige asked as she adjusted her wrought iron café chair.

"Fundraisers, mostly," Sally said. She was a petite redhead with freckles that she didn't try to hide. From a distance, they made her look as if she were still in her twenties. "He was pretty active in local politics for a while."

"Was?"

She shrugged. "I guess he got too busy. I ran into him in Tower Records a few weeks ago, and we got to talking. That's what made me think of you."

"What did?"

Sally smiled. "He was holding one of your books, and I thought, he's wealthy. You're wealthy. He was complaining about how isolating his work was and so were you."

"Isolating? He works for a software company."

"Worked," Sally said. "He's a consultant now, and only when he needs to be. I think he just manages his investments, mostly."

Paige frowned. Had she heard him wrong then? She wasn't paying much attention, not after she had seen the carnations and champagne.

Sally was watching her closely. "I take it things didn't go well."

"He's just not my type."

"Rich? Good-looking? Good God, girl, what is your type?"

Paige smiled. "He's a fan."

"So? Wouldn't that be more appealing?"

Maybe it should have been. Maybe she had over-reacted. She had psyched herself out a number of time about the strange men in the big city. Maybe her over-active imagination—the one that created all the stories that had made her wealthy—had finally betrayed her.

"No," Paige said. "Actually, it's less appealing. I sort of feel like he has photos of me naked and has studied them up close."

"I didn't think books were that personal. I mean, you write romance. That's fantasy, right? Make-believe?"

Paige's smile was thin. It was make-believe. But make-believe on any level had a bit of truth to it, even when little children were creating scenarios with Barbie dolls.

"I just don't think we were compatible," Paige said. "I'm sorry."

Sally shrugged again. "No skin off my nose. You're the one who doesn't get out much. Have you ever thought of going to those singles dinners? They're supposed to be a pretty good place to meet people…"

Paige let the advice slip off her, knowing that she probably wouldn't discuss her love life—or lack of it—with Sally again. Paige had been right in the first place: she simply didn't have the right attitude to be a good blind date. There was probably nothing wrong with Josiah Wells. He had certainly gone to a lot of trouble to make sure she had a good time, and she had snuck off as soon as she could.

And if she couldn't be satisfied with a good-looking wealthy man who was trying to please her, then she wouldn't be satisfied with any other blind date either. She had to go back to that which she knew worked. She had to go about her life normally, and hope that someday, an interesting guy would cross her path.

"…even go to AA to find dates. I mean, that's a little crass, don't you think?"

Paige looked at Sally, and realized she hadn't heard most of Sally's monologue. "You know what? Let's forget about men. It's a brand-new century and I have a great life. Why do we both seem to think that a man will somehow improve that?"

Sally studied her for a moment. "You know what I think? I think you've spent so much time making up the perfect man that no flesh-and-blood guy will measure up."

And then she changed the subject, just like Paige had asked.

***

AS PAIGE DROVE HOME, she found herself wondering if Sally was right. After all, Paige hadn't dated anyone since she quit her job. And that was when she really spent most of her time immersed in imaginary romance. Her conscious brain knew that the men she made up were too perfect to be real. But did her subconscious? Was that what was preventing her from talking to men she'd seen at the opera or the theater? Was all this big city fear she'd been thinking about simply a way of preventing herself from remembering that men were as human—and as imperfect—as she was?

She almost had herself convinced as she parked her new VW Bug on the hill in front of her house. She set the emergency brake and then got out, grabbing her purse as she did.

She had a lot of work to do, and she had wasted most of the day obsessing about her unsatisfying blind date. It was time to return to work—a romantic suspense novel set on a cruise ship. She had done a mountain of research for the book—including two cruises—one to Hawaii in the winter, and another to Alaska in the summer. The Alaska trip was the one she had decided to use, and she had spent part of the spring in Juneau.

By the time she had reached the front porch, she was already thinking of the next scene she had to write. It was a description of Juneau, a city that was perfect for her purposes because there was only two ways out of it: by air or by sea. The roads ended just outside of town. The mountains hemmed everything in, trapping people, good and bad, hero and villain, within their steep walls.

She was so lost in her imagination that she nearly tripped over the basket sitting on her porch.

She bent down to look at it. Wrapped in colored cellophane, it was nearly as large as she was, and was filled with flowers, chocolates, wine and two crystal wine goblets. In the very center was a photo in a heart-shaped gold frame. She peered at it through the wrapping and then recoiled.

It was a picture of her and Josiah at dinner the night before, looking, from the outside, like a very happy couple.

Obviously he had hired someone to take the picture. Someone who had watched them the entire evening, and waited for the right moment to snap the shot. That was unsettling. And so was the fact that Josiah had found her house. She was unlisted in the phonebook, and on public records, she used her first name—Giacinta—with no middle initial. And although her last name was unusual, there were at least five other Racettes listed. Had Josiah sent a basket to every one of them, hoping that he'd find the right one and she'd call him?

Or had he had her followed?

The thought made her look over her shoulder. Maybe there was someone on the street now, watching her, wondering how she would react to this gift.

She didn't want to bring it inside, but she felt like she had no choice. She suddenly felt quite exposed on the porch.

She picked up the basket by its beribboned handle and unlocked her door. Then she stepped inside, closed the door as her security firm had instructed her, and punched in her code. Her hands were shaking.

On impulse, she reset the perimeter alarm. She hadn't done that since she moved in, had thought it a silly precaution.

It didn't seem that silly any more.

She set the basket on the deacons bench she had near the front door. Then she fumbled through the ribbon to find the card which she knew had to be there.

Her name was on the envelope in calligraphed script, but the message inside was typed on the delivery service's card.

Two hearts, perfectly meshed.
Two lives, perfectly twined.
Is it luck that we have found each other?
Or does Fate divine a way for perfect matches to meet?

Those were her words. The stilted words of Quinn Ralston, the hero of her sixth novel, a man who finally learned to free the poetry locked in his soul.

"God," she whispered, so creeped out that her hands felt dirty just from touching the card. She picked up the basket and carried it to the back of the house, setting it in the entryway where she kept her bundled newspapers.

She supposed most women would keep the chocolates, flowers, and wine even if they didn't like the man who sent them. But she wasn't most women. And the photograph bothered her more than she could say.

She locked the interior door, then went to the kitchen and scrubbed her hands until they were raw.

***

SOMEHOW SHE MANAGED to escape to the Juneau of her imagination, working furiously in her upstairs office, getting nearly fifteen pages done before dinner. Uncharacteristically, she closed the drapes, hiding the city view she had paid so much for. She didn't want anyone looking in.

She was cooking herself a taco salad out of Bite-sized Tostitos and bagged shredded lettuce when the phone rang, startling her. She went to answer it, and then some instinct convinced her not to. Instead, she went to her answering machine and turned up the sound.

"Paige? If you're there, please pick up. It's Josiah." He paused and she held her breath. She hadn't given him this number. And Sally had said that morning that she hadn't given Paige's unlisted number to anyone. "Well, um, you're probably working and can't hear this."

A shiver ran through her. He knew she was home, then? Or was he guessing.

"I just wanted to find out of you got my present. I have tickets to tomorrow night's presentation of *La Boheme*. I know how much you love opera and this one in particular. They're box seats. Hard to get. And perfect, just like you. Call me back." He rattled off his phone number and then hung up.

She stared at the machine, with its blinking red light. She hadn't discussed the opera with him. She hadn't discussed the opera with Sally either, after she found out that Sally hated "all that screeching." Sally wouldn't know *La Boheme* from *Don Giovanni*, and she certainly wouldn't remember either well enough to mention to someone else.

Well, maybe Paige's problem was that she had been polite to him the night before. Maybe she should have left. She'd had this problem in the past—mostly in college. She'd always tried to be polite to men who were interested in her, even if she wasn't interested in return. But sometimes, politeness merely encouraged them. Sometimes she had to be harsh just to send them away.

Harsh or polite, she really didn't want to talk to Josiah ever again. She would ignore the call, and hope that he would forget her. Most men understood a lack of response. They knew it for the brush-off it was.

If he managed to run into her, she would just apologize and give him the You're Very Nice I'm Sure You'll Meet Someone Special Someday speech. That one worked every time.

Somehow, having a plan calmed her. She finished cooking the beef for her taco salad and took it to the butcher block table in the center of her kitchen. There she opened the latest copy of *Publisher's Weekly* and read it while she ate.

***

DURING THE NEXT WEEK, she got fifteen bouquets of flowers, each one an arrangement described in her books. Her plan wasn't working. She hadn't run into Josiah, but she didn't answer his phone calls. He didn't seem to understand the brush off. He would call two or three times a day to leave messages on her machine, and once an hour, he would call and hang up. Sometimes she found herself standing over the Caller ID box, fists clenched.

All of this made work impossible. When the phone rang, she listened for his voice. When it wasn't him, she scrambled to pick up, her concentration broken.

In addition to the bouquets, he had taken to sending her cards and writing her long e-mails, sometimes mimicking the language of the men in her novels.

Finally, she called Sally and explained what was going on.

"I'm sorry," Sally said. "I had no idea he was like this."

Paige sighed heavily. She was beginning to feel trapped in the house. "You started this. What do you recommend?"

"I don't know," Sally said. "I'd offer to call him, but I don't think he'll listen to me. This sounds sick."

"Yeah," Paige said. "That's what I'm thinking."

"Maybe you should go to the police."

Paige felt cold. The police. If she went to them, it would be an acknowledgement that this had become serious.

"Maybe," she said, but she hoped she wouldn't have to.

***

LOOKING BACK ON IT, she realized she might have continued enduring if it weren't for the incident at the grocery store. She had been leaving the house, always wondering if someone was watching her, and then deciding that she was being just a bit too paranoid. But the fact that Josiah showed up in the grocery store a few moments after she arrived, pushing no grocery cart and dressed exactly like Maximilian D. Lake from *Love at 37,000 Feet* was no coincidence.

He wore a new brown leather bomber jacket, aviation sunglasses, khakis and a white scarf. When he saw her in the produce aisle, he whipped the sunglasses off with an affected air.

"Paige, darling! I've been worried about you." His eyes were even more intense that she remembered, and this time they were green, just like Maximilian Lake's.

"Josiah," she said, amazed at how calm she sounded. Her heart was pounding and her stomach was churning. He had her trapped—her cart was between the tomato and asparagus aisles. Behind her, the water jets, set to mist the produce every five minutes, kicked on.

"You have no idea how concerned I've been," he said, taking a step closer. She backed toward the onions. "When a person lives alone, works alone, and doesn't answer her phone, well, anything could be wrong."

Was that a threat? She couldn't tell. She made herself smile at him. "There's no need to worry about me. There are people checking on me all the time."

"Really?" He raised a single eyebrow, something she'd often described in her novels, but never actually seen in person. He probably knew that no one came to her house without an invitation. He seemed to know everything else.

She gripped the handle on her shopping cart firmly. "I'm glad I ran into you. I've been wanting to tell you something."

His face lit up, a look that would have been attractive if it weren't so needy. "You have?"

She nodded. Now was the time, her best and only chance. She pushed the cart forward just a little, so that he had to move aside. He seemed to think she was doing it to get closer to him. She was doing it so that she'd be able to get away.

"I really appreciate all the trouble you went to for dinner," she said. "It was one of the most memorable—"

"Our entire life could be like that," he said quickly. "An adventure every day, just like your books."

She had to concentrate to keep that smile on her face. "Writers write about adventure, Josiah, because we really don't want to go out and experience it ourselves."

He laughed. It sounded forced. "I'm sure Papa Hemingway is spinning in his grave. You are such a kidder, Paige."

"I'm not kidding," she said. "You're a very nice man, Josiah, but—"

"A nice man?" He took a step toward her, his face suddenly red. "A nice man? The only men who get described that way in your books are the losers, the ones the heroine wants to let down easy."

She let the words hang between them for a moment. And then she said, "I'm sorry."

He stared at her as if she had hit him. She pushed the cart passed him, resisting the impulse to run. She was rounding the corner into the meat aisle when she heard him say, "You *bitch!*"

Her hands started trembling then, and she couldn't read her list. But she had to. He wouldn't run her out of here. Then he'd realize just how scared she was.

He was coming up behind her. "You can't do this, Paige. You know how good we are together. You know."

She turned around, leaned against her cart and prayed silently for strength. "Josiah, we had one date, and it wasn't very good. Now please, leave me alone."

A store employee was watching from the corner of the aisle. The butcher had looked up through the window in the back.

Josiah grabbed her wrist so hard that she could feel his fingers digging into her skin. "I'll make you remember. I'll make you—"

"Are you all right, miss?" The store employee had stepped to her side.

"No," she said. "He's hurting me."

"This is none of your business," Josiah said. "She's my girlfriend."

"I don't know him," Paige said.

The employee had taken Josiah's arm. Other employees were coming from various parts of the store. He must have given them a signal. Some of the customers were gathering too.

"Sir, we're going to have to ask you to leave," the employee said.

"You have no right."

"We have every right, sir," the employee said. "Now let the lady go."

Josiah stared at him for a moment, then at the other customers. Store security had joined them.

"Paige," Josiah said, "tell them how much you love me. Tell them that we were meant to be together."

"I don't know you," she said, and this time her words seemed to get through. He let go of her arm and allowed the employee to pull him away.

She collapsed against her cart in relief, and the store manager, a middle-aged man with a nice face, asked her if she needed to sit down. She nodded. He led her to the back of the store, past the cans that were being recycled and the gray refrigeration units to a tiny office filled with red signs about customer service.

"I'm sorry," she said. "I'm so sorry."

"Why?" The manager pulled over a metal folding chair and helped her into it. Then he sat behind the desk. "It seemed like he was harassing you. Who is he?"

"I don't really know." She was still shaking. "A friend set us up on a blind date, and he hasn't left me alone since."

"Some friend," the manager said. His phone beeped, and he answered it. He spoke for a moment, his words soft. She didn't listen. She was staring at her wrist. Josiah's fingers had left marks.

Then the manager hung up. "He's gone. Our man took his license number and he's been forbidden to come into the store again. That's all we can do."

"Thank you," she said.

The manager frowned. He was looking at her bruised wrist as well. "You know guys like him don't back down."

"I'm beginning to realize that," she said.

***

AND THAT WAS HOW she found herself parking her grocery-stuffed car in front of the local precinct. It was a gray cinderblock building built in the late 1960s with reinforced windows and a steel door. Somehow it did not inspire confidence.

She went inside anyway. The front hallway was narrow, and obviously redesigned. A steel door stood to her right and to her left was a window made of bullet-proof glass. Behind it sat a man in a police uniform.

She stepped up to the window. He finished typing something into a computer before speaking to her. "What?"

"I'd like to file a complaint."

"I'll buzz you in. Take the second door to your right. Someone there'll help you."

"Thanks," she said, but her voice was lost in the electronic buzz that filled the narrow hallway. She opened the door and found herself in the original corridor, filled with blond wood and doors with windows. Very sixties, very unsafe. She shook her head slightly, opened the second door, and stepped inside.

She entered a large room filled with desks. It smelled of burned coffee and mold. Most of the desks were empty, although on most of them, the desk lamps were on, revealing piles of papers and files. Black phones as old as the building sat on each desk, and she was startled to see that typewriters outnumbered computers.

There were only a handful of people in the room, most of them bent over their files, looking frustrated. A man with salt and pepper hair was carrying a cup of coffee back to his desk. He didn't look like any sort of police detective she'd imagined. He was squarely built and seemed rather ordinary.

When he saw her, he said, "Help you?"

"I want to file a complaint."

"Come with me." His deep voice was cracked and hoarse, as if he had been shouting all day.

He led her to a small desk in the center of the room. Most of the desks were pushed together facing each other, but this one stood alone. And it had a computer, screen showing the SFPD logo.

"I'm Detective Conover. How can I help you, Miss…?"

"Paige Racette." Her voice sounded small in the large room.

He kicked a scarred wooden chair toward her. "What's your complaint?"

She sat down slowly, her heart pounding. "I'm being harassed."

"Harassed?"

"Stalked."

He looked at her straight on, then, and she thought she saw a world-weariness in his brown eyes. His entire face was rumpled, like a coat that had been balled up and left in the bottom of a closet. It wasn't a handsome face by any definition, but it had a comfortable quality, a trustworthy quality, that was built into the lines.

"Tell me about it," he said.

So she did. She started with the blind date, talked about how strange Josiah was, and how he wouldn't leave her alone.

"And he was taking things out of my novels like I would appreciate it. It really upset me."

"Novels?" It was the first time Conover had interrupted her.

She nodded. "I write romances."

"And are you published?"

The question startled her. Usually when she mentioned her name people recognized it. They always recognized it after she said she wrote romances.

"Yes," she said.

"So you were hoisted on your own petard, aren't you?"

"Excuse me?"

"You write about your sexual fantasies for a living, and then complain when someone is trying to take you up on it." He said that so deadpan, so seriously, that for a moment, she couldn't breathe.

"It's not like that," she said.

"Oh? It's advertising, lady."

She was shaking again. She had known this was a bad idea. Why would she expect sympathy from the police? "So since Donald Westlake writes about thieves, he shouldn't complain if he gets robbed? Or Stephen King shouldn't be upset if someone breaks his ankle with a sledgehammer?"

"Touchy," the detective said, but she noticed a twinkle in his eye that hadn't been there before.

She actually counted to ten, silently, before responding. She hadn't done that since she was a little girl. Then she said, as calmly as she could, "You baited me on purpose."

He grinned—and it smoothed out the care lines in his face, enhancing the twinkle in his eye and, for a moment, making him breathlessly attractive.

"There are a lot of celebrities in this town, Ms. Racette. It's hard for the lesser ones to get noticed. Sometimes they'll stage some sort of crime for publicity's sake.

And really, what would be better than a romance writer being romanced by a fan who was using the structure of her books to do it?"

She wasn't sure what she objected to the most, being called a minor celebrity, being branded as a publicity hound, or finding this outrageous man attractive, even for a moment.

"I don't like attention," she said slowly. "If I liked attention, I would have chosen a different career. I hate book signings and television interviews, and I certainly don't want a word of this mess breathed to the press."

"So far so good," he said. She couldn't tell if he believed her, still. But she was amusing him. And that really pissed her off.

She held up her wrist. "He did this."

The smile left Conover's face. He took her hand gently in his own and extended it, examining the bruises as if they were clues. "When?"

"About an hour ago. At San Francisco Produce." She flushed saying the name of the grocery store. It was upscale and trendy, precisely the place a "celebrity" would shop.

But Conover didn't seem to notice. "You didn't tell me about the attack."

"I was getting to it when you interrupted me," she said. "I've been getting calls from him—a dozen or more a day. Flowers, presents, letters and e-mails. I'm unlisted and I never gave him my phone number or my address. I have a private e-mail address, not the one my publisher hands out, and that's the one he's using. And then he followed me to the grocery store and got angry when the store security asked him to leave."

Conover eased her hand onto his desk, then leaned back in his chair. His touch had been gentle, and she missed it.

"You had a date with him—"

"A blind date. We met at the restaurant, and a friend handled the details. And no, she didn't give him the information either."

"—so," Conover said, as if she hadn't spoken, "I assume you know his name."

"Josiah Wells."

Conover wrote it down. Then he sighed. It looked like he was gathering himself. "You have a stalker, Ms. Racette."

"I know."

"And while stalking is illegal under California law, the law is damned inadequate. I'll get the video camera tape from the store, and if it backs you up, I'll arrest Wells. You'll be willing to press charges?"

"Yes," she said.

"That's a start." Conover's world-weary eyes met hers. "but I have to be honest. Usually these guys get out on bail. You'll need a lawyer to get an injunction against him, and your guy will probably ignore it. Even if he gets sent up for a few years, he'll come back and haunt you. They always do."

Her shaking started again. "So what can I do?"

"Your job isn't tied to the community. You can move."

Move? She felt cold. "I have a house." A life. This was her dream city. "I don't want to move."

"No one does, but it's usually the only thing that works."

"I don't want to run away," she said. "If I do that, then he'll be controlling my life. I'd be giving in. I'd be a victim."

Conover stared at her for a long moment. "Tell you what. I'll build the strongest case I can. That might give you a few years. By then, you might be willing to go somewhere new."

She nodded, stood. "I'll bring everything in tomorrow."

"I'd like to pick it up, if you don't mind. See where he left it, whether he's got a hidey hole near the house. How about I come to you in a couple of hours?"

"Okay," she said.

"You got a peephole?"

"Yeah."

"Use it. I'll knock."

She nodded. Then felt her shoulders relax slightly, more than they had for two weeks. Finally, she had an ally. It meant more to her than she had realized it would. "Thanks."

"Don't thank me yet," he said. "Let's wait until this is all over."

All over. She tried to concentrate on the words and not the tone. Because Detective Conover really didn't sound all that optimistic.

***

THE BIGGEST BOUQUET waited for her on the front porch. She could see it from the street, and any hope that the meeting with Conover aroused disappeared.

She knew without getting out of the car what the bouquet would be: calla lilies, tiger lilies and Easter lilies, mixed with greens and lilies of the valley. It was a bouquet Marybeth Campbell was designing the day she met Robert Newman in *All My Kisses*, a bouquet he said was both romantic and sad. (Not to mention expensive: the flowers weren't in season at the same time.)

She left the bouquet on the porch without reading the card. Conover would be there soon and he could take the whole mess away. She certainly didn't want to look at it.

After all this, she wasn't sure she ever wanted to see flowers again.

When she got inside, she found twenty-three messages on her machine, all from Josiah, all apologies, although they got angrier and angrier as she didn't answer. He must have thought she had come straight home. What a surprise he would have when he realized that she had gone to the police.

She rubbed her wrist, noting the soreness and cursing him under her breath. In addition to the bruises, her wrist was slightly swollen and she wondered if he hadn't managed to sprain it. Just her luck. He would damage her arm, which she needed to write. She got an ice pack out of the freezer and applied it, sitting at the kitchen table and staring at nothing.

Move. Give up, give in, all because she was feeling lonely and wanted to go on a date. All because she wanted a little flattery, a nice evening, to meet someone safe who could be—if nothing else—a friend.

How big a mistake had that been?

Big enough, she was beginning to realize, to cost her everything she held dear.

***

THAT NIGHT, AFTER DINNER, she baked herself a chocolate cake and covered it with marshmallow frosting. It was her grandmother's recipe—comfort food that Paige normally never allowed herself. This time, though, she would eat the whole thing and not worry about calories or how bad it looked. Who would know?

She made some coffee and was sitting down to a large piece, when someone knocked on her door.

She got up and walked to the door, feeling oddly vulnerable. If it was Josiah, he would only be a piece of wood away from her. That was too close. It was all too close now.

She peered through the peephole, just like she promised Conover she would, and she let out a small sigh of relief. He was shifting from foot to foot, looking down at the bouquet she had forgotten she had left there.

She deactivated the security system, then unlocked the three deadbolts and the chain lock she had installed since this nightmare began. Conover shoved the bouquet forward with his foot.

"Looks like your friend left another calling card."

"He's not my friend," she said softly, peering over Conover's shoulder. "And he left more than that."

Conover's glance was worried. What did he imagine?

"Phone calls," she said. "Almost two dozen. I haven't checked my e-mail."

"This guy's farther along than I thought." Conover pushed the bouquet all the way inside with his foot, then closed the door, and locked it. As he did, she reset the perimeter alarm.

Conover slipped on a pair of gloves and picked up the bouquet.

"You could have done that outside," she said.

"Didn't want to give him the satisfaction," Conover said. "He has to know we don't respect what he's doing. Where can I look at this?"

"Kitchen," she said, pointing the way.

He started toward it, then stopped, sniffing. "What smells so good?"

"Chocolate cake. You want some?"

"I thought you wrote."

"Doesn't stop me from baking on occasion."

He glanced at her, his dark eyes quizzical. "This hardly seems the time to be baking."

She shrugged. "I could drink instead."

To her surprise, he laughed. "Yes, I guess you could."

He carried the bouquet into the kitchen and set it on a chair. Then he dug through the flowers to find the card.

It was a different picture of their date. The photograph looked professional, almost artistic, done in black and white, using the light from the candles to illuminate her face. At first glance, she seemed entranced with Josiah. But when she looked closely, she could see the discomfort on her face.

"You didn't like him much," Conover said.

"He was creepy from the start, but in subtle hard-to-explain ways."

"Why didn't you leave?"

"I was raised to be polite. I had no idea he was crazy."

Conover grunted at that. He opened the card. The handwriting inside was the same as all the others.

My future and your future are the same. You are my heart and soul. Without you, I am nothing.
                                                    —Josiah

She closed her eyes, felt that fluttery fear rise in her again. "There'll be a ring somewhere in that bouquet."

"How do you know?" Conover asked.

She opened her eyes. "Go look at the last page of *All My Kisses*. Robert sends a forgive-me bouquet and in it, he puts a diamond engagement ring."

"This bouquet?"

"No. Josiah already used that one. I guess he thought this one is more spectacular."

Conover dug, and then whistled. There, among the stems, was a black velvet ring box. He opened it. A large diamond glittered against a circle of sapphires in a white gold setting.

"Jesus," he said. "I could retire on this thing."

"I always thought that was a gaudy ring," Paige said, her voice shaking. "But it fit the characters."

"Not to your taste?"

"No." She sighed and sank back into her chair. "Just because I write about it doesn't mean I want it to happen to me."

"I think you made that clear in the precinct today." He put the ring box back where he found it, returned the card to its envelope and set the flowers on the floor. "Mind if I have some of that cake?"

"Oh, I'm sorry." She got up and cut him a piece of cake, then poured some coffee.

When she turned around, he was grinning.

"What did I do?" she asked.

"You weren't kidding about polite," he said. "I didn't come here for a tea party, and you could have said no."

She froze in place. "Was this another of your tests? To see if I was really that polite?"

"I wish I were that smart." He took the plate from her hand. "I was getting knocked out by the smell. My mother used to make this cake. It always was my favorite."

"With marshmallow frosting?"

"And that spritz of melted chocolate on top, just like you have here." He set the plate down and took the coffee from her hand. "Although in those days, I would have preferred a large glass of milk."

"I have some—"

"Sit." If anything, his grin had gotten bigger. "Forgive me for being so blunt, but what the hell did you need with a blind date?"

There was admiration in his eyes—real admiration, not the sick kind she'd seen from Josiah. She used her fork to cut a bite of cake. "I was lonely. I don't get out much, and I thought, what could it hurt?"

He shook his head. That weary look had returned to his face. She liked its rumpled quality, the way that he seemed to be able to take the weight of the world onto himself and still stand up. "What a way to get disillusioned."

"Because I'm a romance writer?"

"Because you're a person."

They ate the cake in silence after that, then he gripped his coffee mug and leaned back in the chair.

"Thanks," he said. "I'd forgotten that little taste of childhood."

"There's more."

"Maybe later." And there was no smile on his face any more, no enjoyment. "I have to tell you a few things."

She pushed her own plate away.

"I looked up Josiah Wells. He's got a sheet."

She grabbed her own coffee cup. It was warm and comforting. "Let me guess. The political conferences he stopped going to."

Conover frowned at her. "What conferences?"

"Here in San Francisco. He was active in local politics. That's how my friend Sally met him."

"And he stopped?"

"Rather suddenly. I thought, after all this started, that maybe—"

"I'll check into it," Conover said with a determination she hadn't heard from him before. "His sheet's from San Diego."

"I thought he was from here."

Conover shook his head. "He's not a dot-com millionaire. He made his money on a software system back in the early nineties, before everyone was into this business. Sold his interest for 30 million dollars and some stock, which has since risen in value. About ten times what it was."

Her mouth had gone dry. Josiah Wells had lied to both her and Sally. "Somehow I suspect this is important."

"Yeah." Conover took a sip of coffee. "He stalked a woman in San Diego."

"Oh, God." The news gave her a little too much relief. She had been feeling alone. But she didn't want anyone else to be experiencing the same thing she was.

"He killed her."

"What?" Paige froze.

"When she resisted him, he shot her and killed her." Conover's soft gaze was on her now, measuring. All her relief had vanished. She was suddenly more terrified than she had ever been.

"You know it was him?"

"I read the file. They faxed it to me this afternoon. All of it. They had him one hundred percent. DNA matches, semen matches—"

She winced, knowing what that meant.

"—the fibers from his home on her clothing, and a list of stalking complaints and injunctions that went on for pages."

The cake sat like a lump in her stomach. "Then why isn't he in prison?"

"Money," Conover said. "His attorneys so out-classed the DA's office that by the end of the trial, they could have convinced the jury that the judge had done it."

"Oh, my god," Paige said.

"The same things that happened to you happened to her," Conover said. "Only with her those things took about two years. With you it's taking two weeks."

"Because he feels like he knows me from my books?"

Conover shook his head. "She was a TV business reporter who had done an interview with him. He would have felt like he knew her too."

"What then?" Somehow having the answer to all of that would make her feel better—or maybe she was just lying to herself.

"These guys are like alcoholics. If you take a guy through AA, and keep him sober for a year, then give him a drink, he won't rebuild his drinking career from scratch. He'll start at precisely the point he left off."

She had to swallow hard to keep the cake down. "You think she wasn't the only one."

"Yeah. I suspect if we look hard enough, we'll find a trail of women, each representing a point in the escalation of his sickness."

"You can arrest him, right?"

"Yes." Conover spoke softly. "But only on what he's done. Not on what he might do. And I don't think we'll be any more successful at holding him than the San Diego DA."

Paige ran her hand over the butcher block table. "I have to leave, don't I?"

"Yeah." Conover's voice got even softer. He put a hand on hers. She looked at him. It wasn't world-weariness in his eyes. It was sadness. Sadness from all the things he'd seen, all the things he couldn't change.

"I'm from a small town," she said. "I don't want to bring him there."

"Is there anywhere else you can go? Somewhere he wouldn't think of?"

"New York," she said. "I have friends I can stay with for a few weeks."

"This'll take longer than a few weeks. You might not be able to come back."

"I know. But that'll give me time to find a place to live." Her voice broke on that last. This had been her dream city, her dream home. How quickly that vanished.

"I'm sorry," he said.

"Yeah," she said quietly. "Me, too."

***

HE DECIDED TO STAY without her asking him. He said he wanted to sift through the evidence, listen to the phone messages, and read the e-mail. She printed off all of it while she bought plane tickets on-line. Then she e-mailed her agent and told her that she was coming to the City.

Already she was talking like the New Yorker she was going to be.

Her flight left at 8 a.m. She spent half the night packing and unpacking, uncertain about what she would need, what she should leave behind. The only thing she was certain about was that she would need her laptop, and she spent an hour loading her files onto it. She was writing down the names of some moving and packing services when Conover stopped her.

"We leave everything as is," he said. "We don't want him to get too suspicious too soon."

"Why don't you arrest him now?" she asked. "Don't you have enough?"

Something flashed across his face, so quickly she almost didn't catch it.

"What?" she asked. "What is it?"

He closed his eyes. If anything, that made his face look even more rumpled. "I issued a warrant for his arrest before I came here. We haven't found him yet."

"Oh, God." Paige slipped into her favorite chair. One of many things she would have to leave behind, one of many things she might never see again because of Josiah Wells.

"We have people watching his house, watching yours, and a few other places he's known to hang out," Conover said. "We'll get him soon enough."

She nodded, trying to look reassured, even though she wasn't.

***

About 3 a.m., Conover looked at her suitcases sitting in the middle of the dining room floor. "I'll have to ship those to you. No sense tipping him off if he's watching this place."

"I thought you said—"

"I did. But we need to be careful. One duffel. The rest can wait."

"My laptop," she said. "I need that too."

He sighed. "All right. The laptop and the biggest purse you have. Nothing more."

A few hours earlier, she might have argued with him. But a few hours earlier, she hadn't yet gone numb.

"I need some sleep," she said.

"I'll wake you," he said, "when it's time to go."

* * *

HE DROVE HER to the airport in his car. It was an old bathtub Porsche—with the early seventies bucket seats that were nearly impossible to get into.

"She's not pretty any more," he said as he tucked Paige's laptop behind the seat, "but she can move."

They left at 5, not so much as to miss traffic, but hoping that Wells wouldn't be paying attention at that hour. Conover also kept checking his rearview mirror, and a few times he executed some odd maneuvers.

"We being followed?" she asked finally.

"I don't think so," he said. "But I'm being cautious."

His words hung between them. She watched the scenery go by, houses after houses after houses filled with people who went about their ordinary lives, not worrying about stalkers or death or losing everything.

"This isn't normal for you, is it?" she asked after a moment.

"Being cautious?" he said. "Of course it is."

"No." Paige spoke softly. "Taking care of someone like this."

He seemed even more intent on the road than he had been. "All cases are different."

"Really?"

He turned to her, opened his mouth, and then closed it again, sighing. "Josiah Wells is a predator."

"I know," she said.

"We have to do what we can to catch him." His tone was odd. She frowned. Was that an apology for something she didn't understand? Or an explanation for his attentiveness?

Maybe it was both.

He turned onto the road leading to San Francisco International Airport. The traffic seemed even thicker here, through all the construction and the dust. It seemed like they were constantly remodeling the place. Somehow he made it through the confusing signs to Short Term Parking. He found a space, parked, and then grabbed her laptop from the back.

"You're coming in?" she asked.

"I want to see you get on that plane." He seemed oddly determined.

"Don't you trust me?"

"Of course I do," he said and got out of the car.

San Francisco International Airport was an old airport, built right on the bay. The airport had been trying to modernize for years. The new parts were grafted on like artificial limbs.

Paige took a deep breath, grabbed her stuffed over-sized purse, and let Conover lead her inside. She supposed they looked like any couple as they went through the automatic doors, stopping to examine the signs above them pointing to the proper airline. Conover was watching the other passengers. Paige was checking out the lines.

She had bought herself a first class ticket—spending more money than she had spent for her very first car. But she was leaving everything behind. The last thing she wanted was to be crammed into couch next to a howling baby and an underpaid, stressed businessman.

She hurried to the first class line, relieved that it was short. Conover stayed beside her, frowning as he watched the people flow past. He seemed both disappointed and alert. He was expecting something. But what?

Paige stepped to the ticket counter, gave her name, showed her identification, answered the silly security questions, and got her E-ticket with the gate number written on the front.

"You've got an hour and a half," Conover said as she left the ticket counter. "Let's get breakfast."

His hand rested possessively on her elbow, and he pulled her close as he spoke. She glanced at him, but he still wasn't watching her.

"I have to make a stop first," she said.

He nodded.

They walked past the arrival and departure monitors, past the newspaper vending machines and toward the nearest restrooms. This part of the San Francisco airport still had a seventies security design. Instead of a bank of x-ray machines and metal detectors blocking entry into the main part of the terminal, there was nothing. The security measures were in front of each gate: you couldn't enter without going past a security checkpoint. So different from New York, where you couldn't even walk into some areas without a ticket. Conover would have no trouble remaining beside her until it was time for her to take off.

She went into the ladies room, leaving Conover near the departure monitors outside. The line was long—several flights had just arrived—but Paige didn't mind. This was the first time she had a moment to herself since Conover had arrived the night before.

It seemed like weeks ago.

She was going to be sorry to say good-bye to him at the gate. In that short period of time, she had come to rely on him more than she wanted to admit. He made her feel safe for the first time since she had met Josiah Wells.

As she exited the ladies room, a hand grabbed her arm and pulled her sideways. She felt something poke against her back.

"Think you could leave me?"

Wells. She shook her arm, trying to get away, but he clamped harder.

"Scream," he said, "and I will hurt you."

"You can't hurt me," she said. "You can't have weapons in an airport."

"You can bring a gun into an airport," he said softly, right in her ear. "You just can't take it through security."

She felt cold then. He was as crazy as Conover said, then. And as dangerous.

"Josiah." She spoke loudly, hoping that Conover could hear her. She didn't see him anywhere. "I'm going to New York on business. When I come back, we can start planning the wedding."

Wells was silent for a moment. He didn't move at all. She couldn't see his face, but she could feel his body go rigid. "You're playing with me."

"No," she said, letting her voice work for her, hoping it sounded convincing. She kept scanning the crowd, but Conover was gone. "I got your ring last night. I decided I needed to settle a few things in New York before I told you I'd say yes."

Wells put his chin on her shoulder. His breath blew against her hair. "You're not wearing the ring."

"It didn't fit." she said. "But I have it with me. I was going to have it sized in New York."

"Let me see it," he said.

"You'll have to let me dig into my purse."

She wasn't sure he'd believe her. Then, after a moment, he let her go. She brought up her purse, pretended to rummage through it, and took a step toward the ladies room door, praying her plan would work.

He was frowning. He looked like any other businessman in the airport, his suit neat and well tailoredwell-tailored, his trench coat long and expensive, marred only by the way he held his hand in the pocket.

She waited just a split second, until there were a lot of people around from another arriving plane, and then she screamed, "He's got a gun!" and ran toward the ladies room.

Only she didn't make it. She was tackled from behind, and went sprawling across the faded carpet. A gunshot echoed around her, and people started screaming, running. The body on top of hers prevented her from moving, and for a moment, she thought whoever had hit her had been shot.

Then she felt arms around her, dragging her toward the departure monitors.

"You little fool," Conover said in her ear. "I had this under control."

He pushed her against the base of the monitor, then turned around. Half the people around Wells had remained, and two of them had him in their grasp, while another was handcuffing him. Plainclothes airport police officers. More airport police were hurrying to the spot from the front door.

Passengers were still screaming and running out of the airport. Airline personnel were crouched behind their desks. Paige looked to see whether anyone was shot, but she didn't see anyone lying injured anywhere.

Her breathing was shallow, and she suddenly realized how terrified she had been. "What do you mean, under control? This doesn't look under control to me."

Security had Wells against the wall and were searching him for more weapons. One of the uniformed airport police had pulled Wells' head back and was yelling at him. Some of the passengers, realizing the threat was over, were drifting back toward the action.

Conover kept one hand on her, holding her in place. With the other, he pulled out his cell phone. He hit the speed-dial and put the small phone against his ear.

"Wait a minute!" Paige said.

He turned away slightly, as if he didn't want to speak to her. Then he said into the phone, "Frank, do me a favor. Call the news media—everyone you can think of. Tell them something just happened at the airport…. No. I'm not going through official channels. That's why I called you. Keep my name out of it and get them here."

He hung up and glanced at Paige. She had never felt so many emotions in her life. Anger, adrenaline, confusion. Then she saw security lead Wells away.

Conover took her arm and helped her up. "What's going on?" she asked again.

"Outside," he said, and pushed her through the crowd. After a moment, she remembered to check for her laptop. He had it, and somehow she had retained her purse. They reached the front sidewalk only to find it a confusion of milling people—some still terrified from the shots, others just arriving and trying to drop off their luggage. Cabs honked and nearly missed each other. Buses were backing up as the crowd spilled into the street.

"Oh, this is so much better," she said.

He moved her down the sidewalk toward another terminal. The crowd thinned here.

"What the hell was that?" she asked. "Where were you? How did he get past you?"

"He didn't get past me," Conover said softly.

She felt the blood leave her face. "You set me up? I was bait?"

"It wasn't supposed to happen like this."

"Oh, really? He was supposed to drag me onto the nearest flight? Or shoot me?"

"I didn't know he had a gun," Conover said. "He was ballsier than I expected. And he wouldn't have taken you from San Francisco."

"You know this how? Because you're psychic?"

"No, he wanted to control you. He couldn't control you on a plane. I had security waiting outside. A few plainclothes had been around us since we arrived. He was supposed to grab you, but you weren't supposed to try to get away."

"Nice if you would have told me that."

He shook his head slightly. "Most people wouldn't have fought him. Most people would have cooperated."

"Most people would have appreciated an explanation!" Her voice rose and a few stray passengers looked her direction. She made herself take a deep breath before she went on. "You knew he was going to be here. You knew it and didn't tell me."

"I guessed," he said.

"What did you do, tip him off?"

"No," Conover said softly. "You did."

"I did? I didn't talk to him."

"You booked your e-ticket online." His face was close to hers, his voice as soft as possible in all the noise. "He'd hacked into your system weeks ago. That's how he found your address and your phone number. Your public e-mail comes into the same computer as all your other e-mail. He's been following your every move ever since."

"Software genius," she muttered, shaking her head. She should have seen that.

Conover nodded. Across the way, reporters started converging on the building, cameras hefted on shoulders, running toward the doors. Conover shielded her, but she knew they would want to talk to her.

"Why didn't you warn me?" she asked again.

"I thought you'd be too obvious then, and he wouldn't try for you. I didn't expect you to be so cool under pressure. Telling him about the ring, pretending you were interested, was smart."

One of the reporters was working the crowd. People were turning toward the camera.

"Where were you?" she asked. "I looked for you."

"I was behind you all the time."

"So if he took me outside…?"

"I would have followed."

"I don't understand. Why didn't you tell me not to get the ticket on line?"

"The ticket was a gift," Conover said. "I didn't realize you were going to do it that way. You told me when you finished. His file from the previous case mentioned how he had used the internet to spy on his first victim. He was obviously doing that with you."

"But the airport, how did they know?"

"I called ahead, said that I was coming in, expecting a difficult passenger. I faxed his photo from your place while you were asleep. I asked them to wait until I got him outside, unless he did something threatening."

She frowned. More reporters were approaching. These looked like print media. No cameras, but lots of determination. "You could have waited and caught him at home."

"I could have," Conover said. "But this is better."

She turned to him, remembering the feel of the gun against her back, the screaming passengers, the explosive sound when the gun went off. "Someone could have been killed."

"I didn't expect a gun," Conover said. "And I didn't think he'd be rash enough to use it in an airport."

"But he did," she said.

"And it's going to help us." Conover watched another set of reporters run into the building. "First, his assault on you in an airport makes it a federal case. The gun adds to the case, and all the witnesses make it even better. Then there is the fact that airports are filled with security cameras. There's bound to be tape on this."

She frowned, trying to take herself out of this, trying to listen like a writer instead of a potential victim.

"And then," Conover said, "he attacked you. You're nationally known. It'll be big news. Our DA might have lost a stalking case against Wells, but the feds aren't going to let a guy who went nuts in an airport walk, no matter how much money he has."

"You set him up," she said. "If this had failed—"

"At the very least, I would have been fired," Conover said. "But it wouldn't have failed. I wouldn't have let anything happen to you. I didn't let anything happen to you."

"But you took such a risk." She raised her head toward his. "Why?"

He put a finger under her chin, and for a moment, she thought he was going to kiss her.

"Because you didn't want to leave San Francisco," he said softly.

"I get to stay home?" she asked.

He smiled, and let his finger drop. "Yeah."

He stared at her uncertainly, as if he were afraid she was going to yell at him again. But she felt a relief so powerful that it completely overwhelmed her.

She threw her arms around him. For a moment, he didn't move. Then, slowly, his arms wrapped around her and pulled her close.

"I don't even know your first name," she whispered.

"Pete," he said, burying his face in her hair.

"Pete." She tested it. "It suits you."

"I'd ask if I could call you," he said, "but I'm not real good on dates."

That pulled a reluctant laugh from her. "Obviously I'm not either. But I make a mean chocolate cake."

"That's right," he said. "Let's go finish it."

"Don't we have to talk to the press?"

"For a moment." He pulled back just enough to smile at her. "And then I get to take you home."

"Where I get to stay." She couldn't convey how much this meant to her. "Thank you."

He nodded. "My pleasure."

She leaned her head against his shoulder, feeling his strength, feeling the comfort. It didn't matter how he looked or whether he knew *La Boheme* from *Don Giovanni*. All that mattered was how he made her feel.

Safe. Appreciated. And maybe even loved.

Ghosts

*I*T GOES LIKE THIS:

Fifteen layers between him and the client. His people mostly, from the front that gets the order to the hacker who checks it out. Not everyone who wants to hire a hit man should be to find him. That's why there's redundancy upon redundancy—for every hacker, there's another who double- and triple-checks. After all, he's not going to risk his life, his freedom, on the word of some nobody with a computer, a nobody he's never met.

The order comes through the system—or system*s* if he wants to be more accurate—and if all the information matches, he considers the job. The timetable is necessarily flexible: anyone who wants a quickie goes somewhere else. Quickies get a man in trouble. Check the evening news. Any time a pro gets caught, it's someone who specializes in quickies. Sure, they get top dollar, but they also take maximum risk.

He tries to eliminate risk. He's Aries with Virgo Rising, Moon in Libra. Born for his job, at least according to his chart. Perceived as detail-oriented, almost fussy, a painstaking perfectionist, he is at heart a warrior, brave, impetuous and independent. His true self, his emotional self, is a judge, coldly calculating, always striving for balance.

He has a superstitious side as well, and isn't sure where it comes from. In the past, he tried to bury it, but he finally gave in ten years ago and his business improved.

That was when he discovered Glenna. She had a New Age bookstore in Sedona, Arizona, and an uncanny knack of seeing his future. The first time he entered her store, intrigued by a book in the window, she'd said from her table in the back, "Should I be afraid for myself, old friend?"

The question had both startled and intrigued him, and when he answered no, she smiled and said, "My chart was uncertain. It told me that today would introduce me to Death."

He hadn't heard of a chart, knew nothing about astrology except for the goofy write-ups in the newspapers, write-ups which never seemed to be about him. But she had encouraged him to have his chart done and after careful consideration, he'd given her his birth date, time, and location. She promised to have a reading for him in three days.

It was that reading which changed his life, and added one more layer between him and a job.

Now he compares his client's chart, the chart of his intended victim, and his own chart, searching for the optimum day, the appropriate venue, and of course, any hint of failure. If he's not compatible with a client, he passes the work to someone else. If his read of the victim's chart makes the victim seem personally powerful, dominant over him, or just plain lucky, he passes on that job as well.

He has learned, through trial and error, that he is not right for every job, nor is every job right for him. His perfectionism serves him well, and protects him from his impetuous nature.

He has achieved balance which, for him, makes everything right with the world.

**

THE BALANCE STARTS to crumble on the fourth of May. He is in Los Angeles, using the name Carlisle because it intrigues him. He uses it as a first name because he has learned that people cannot remember an unusual first name. They remember what it sounds like—"I think it was Carl." "No, honey. He called himself Lyle."—not what it is. By the time the police are talking to them, he's long gone, vanished like smoke in a strong wind.

He has his network of astrologers, mostly because he believes in backups, but he never has the network handle all three things—the client's chart, his chart, and the victim's chart. Only Glenna gets all three. She is his double-check, partly because she is so very accurate, and partly because he trusts her as much as he can trust anyone.

She has never worried about who he is or what he does. When she realized what he did for a living, she did not call the police as some would have nor did she suddenly fear him. Her manner toward him did not seem to change.

The afternoon he came for his reading, she greeted him with a smile. "My chart had been right," she said. "I did meet Death yesterday, just not in the way I thought."

It had been his first lesson about horoscopes and charts. When they were done by a true professional, like Glenna, they were incredibly accurate, although, at times, useless. Sometimes the language was too cryptic, too given to misinterpretation.

He learned, through trial and error, to plan his jobs based solely on things he understood—good days, bad days, luck, and the possibility of a future.

The victim's charts were always the easiest to read. If they did not predict a major calamity within a year of the reading, then he did not take the job. He usually appeared in a person's chart as a defining event or a crisis or as Glenna would say, "A possible ending."

The first time she saw one of those in a victim's chart, she made him swear he would not tell the victim.

"I can't promise that," he had said. "But I can promise that I will not give that person false hope."

She had shaken her head at him, but had said nothing. That was when he had asked her why his work didn't bother her.

"I never said that." She folded her hands gravely over the victim's chart. "I vowed, when I went into this business, that I would not judge."

He did not tell her—indeed, he has never told her—that she made his work easier. He feels that is too much information. She probably knows it anyway, since she seems to know everything. But he does not want to take the risk of losing her. She is one of the few sure things in his life.

But he has never been long on trust, which is why he finds himself in a shop that smells of hairspray and plastic, just off Hollywood Boulevard, in the low-rent section of town. The shop has a giant hand in the window—the place is best known for its palm reader who is, in his opinion, a charlatan.

He comes for the astrologer, a pot-smoking eighteen-year-old who calls herself Elli May. She does a weekly or monthly chart for him whenever he comes to Los Angeles. The first time she saw his natal chart, she asked him if he was a cop or a private detective. She clearly lacked the life experience that Glenna had.

"I do work in enforcement," he had said, and left it at that. From that point on, Elli May never questioned him. She also stopped offering him joints.

Her charts are deceptively simple. She uses a computer program which her younger sister designed. She has not customized a chart for him because he hasn't asked her to. He wants to seem as normal as possible, given that he's a hit man visiting a teenage astrologer to find out the best date for his next job.

The shop's hairspray and plastic smell comes from the room deodorizer she uses to cover up the sickly sweet stench of pot. She hasn't yet learned the value of incense.

The palm reader should know—she's old enough to be the girl's grandmother—but she doesn't seem to care. Or maybe she recognizes what the girl does not: that the only law he follows is the one he makes up himself.

"Hey ya," Elli May says when she sees him. She pops a stick of Juicy Fruit and chomps, mouth open. "Didn't think I'd see you today."

Instantly his guard is up. She knew she would see him today. They have an appointment.

"Why's that?" he asks, heading toward her tiny velvet covered table in the back.

Elli May shrugs. She's not a very good liar either. "I'm not really ready for you today, Mr. Carlson."

Here he's Carlson, on the street he's Carlisle. An easy mistake, he'll tell someone if they ever ask. The names sound alike and he's never bothered to correct her—no sense letting the girl know she's wrong.

He slips into the chair, stretching his long legs and resting his hands on his stomach, pretending at an ease he no longer feels. "I think you're ready. I think the chart shows something you don't want to mention."

She flushes a blotchy red. "I don't—"

"You may as well tell me," he says. "You gotta get used to telling clients good news as well as bad."

The palm reader harrumphs behind him, then gets up and grabs her purse. "Want some coffee or something?" she asks Elli May.

"No," Elli May says, her eyes big and pleading. He can read them, probably better than the palm reader can read palms: *Stay. Please stay. He's a scary man and I have bad news.*

"Be back soon," the palm reader says, and heads out. The door bangs behind her.

Elli May looks at him, and swallows, then coughs. He'd bet all the money in his wallet that she has just swallowed her gum.

"It can't be that bad, kid," he says, mostly because he wants out of here, but not without knowing what she knows. "Let's get it over with and you can get back to your smoke."

She squints at him, measuring him in an entirely different way. This is their last time together and she has just begun to understand that he knows it too.

As she slides around the table, she slips a hand in the pocket of her jeans and pulls out another piece of gum. She doesn't offer him any. She takes the stick from the foil, and shoves the gum in her mouth.

Then she sits down, pulls open a drawer, and his chart comes out. It looks like all the others—a wheel with meaningless notations in the outer rim, more symbols between the spokes, and numbers in the inner rim. The numbers are attached by lines that all seem to bunch up in one area. Glenna once told him that this part of his natal chart shows all his strengths. He supposes it also shows his weaknesses.

Elle May sets the chart in front of him.

"Doll," he says because he knows it'll annoy her, "you've already read my natal chart. I asked you for this week."

She wears rings on all of her fingers, including her thumbs, big cheap rings that hid her skin. She toys with one of them now, as if considering what to do next, then she reaches in the drawer and pulls out another chart.

Elli May calls this an action table, and in it are little boxes for inane things like "The Best Time to Take a Vacation" and "The Best Time to Obtain a Loan."

He slides his hand under the new sheet and grabs the natal chart. He sets it on top of the action table and taps it. "Look at all that focus on the Eighth House. What is that again?"

"Finances," she mutters.

"And secrets, mysteries, power, death, and transformation, right?"

She nods.

"Don't fuck with me," he says in a very flat voice. "You give me what I asked for and I'll remember you're just a kid who's learning her job."

Her eyes widen. She folds those ringed hands together. "I, um, threw it away."

"I'm sure you did," he says. "But you remember it."

She bites her chapped lower lip. "Mr. Carlson, please, my aunt—" Apparently that was the palm reader "—she says not to tell everything. It's not smart."

"Usually it's not," he says. "But I'm not your average customer. Did you know that President Reagan, he had an astrologer?"

The girl swallows again, but as she does, she pushes the gum into her cheek where it becomes a bulging, unattractive lump. She's too young to remember Reagan. She was born during his second term. He's just a name from a dusty textbook to her.

"I'll bet that astrologer told him he was gonna get elected the first time. But you think the astrologer tells him that something cataclysmic is gonna happen on March 30, 1981? Probably not. Afraid, you know, that he'll get upset at the reading. So he don't know he's in any danger, any more than usual. That day, he gets out of his car, and wham! shot through the lung by a kid barely outta college. Lives, no thanks to his astrologer. And I'm sure that chart disappeared like nobody's business, and the astrologer says 'No one can anticipate such random events, Mr. President.'"

The girl's blotchy flush gets deeper. He knows he's got her. He had her with the word "cataclysmic," but he went on because she was young and needed to hear the point. Not for him. He's not coming here again—he doesn't like working this hard, not with one of his people—but maybe for someone else.

Occasionally, he can be altruistic, although it always surprises him. He thinks it may come from his Rising Sign. Virgos are known to be helpful at times.

She reaches into the drawer a third time, and pulls out a computer-generated sheet filled with squiggles and symbols he does not understand. The week's dates are running along the side, May 4-11. That's the only part he recognizes.

He hides his surprise; he was so convinced she had destroyed this that he almost doesn't believe it's before him.

"Okay," he says, leaning forward. "Explain it to me."

"It's called a termination event." Her voice is shaking. "But it doesn't necessarily mean you're going to die. It means that something significant in your life will end, change, terminate, you know."

"Significant how?" he asks. He knows these charts can pick out various aspects—relationships, home life, business. He needs specifics.

"It threads through everything," she says. "Work, relationships, finances. I've never seen anything like it."

Of course not. She's a baby. She's never seen anything like anything.

"It started this morning, or maybe even a couple of days ago. You didn't have me run that, so I don't know."

And wasn't bright enough to check. He's glad he's not one of the careless types, the kind who uses his power easily. He can just imagine pulling his gun from its shoulder holster beneath his suit jacket, ending this session with a bullet. But he won't, no matter how annoyed he is. He's more of a planner than that.

Besides, he has a hunch this isn't the kind of termination event she's talking about.

"It builds until the sixth, when everything comes to a head, and then, I don't know. The chart flips, and to be honest with you, sir, I haven't seen anything like this."

"Like what?"

"Nothing."

At first he thinks she's being evasive, then he realizes that she means literally nothing.

"How can that be?" he asks.

She shrugs. "I tried calling the guy who trained me, but he's at some retreat in Michigan until the 15th."

He sighs, slaps a fifty on the table, and takes all three charts, even though they're not worth that much.

"Anything else?" he asks as he stands.

"Yeah," she says, standing too, and pointing at the top sheet. "Right now, your energy is at odds with itself. A lot of things will be revealed, secrets will be uncovered. There's so much darkness here that it scares me."

"I suppose it would," he says.

"No." She straightens her shoulders, apparently thinking it makes her look stronger and taller. It actually makes her look scared. "You don't understand. All these things, they're very bad. I've never seen such a horrible chart. If I were you, I'd go to bed and not leave for a week."

"I suppose you would," he says.

Her lips narrow and anger flashes through her eyes. "I'm trying to warn you."

"Of what?" he asks, hoping this time she'll be specific.

"This week," she says, "you may lose everything."

He studies her for a moment. She seems so sincere, so worried about him, even though she doesn't really know him.

"It wouldn't be the first time," he says, and walks out the door.

***

THE FIRST TIME had been twenty years ago. He'd been working as a bouncer at a major New York nightclub, and he'd gotten friendly with the owner, a balding man who wore too much jewelry and liked a little too much blow. He supplied it to his friends, too, and used Ben, as he'd been known then, to deliver it.

Young Ben proved his honesty—he always returned the money, every dime of it, to the club's owner—and his street smarts. He'd thwarted more than one robbery attempt, and he'd beaten a handful of men much larger than himself to a bloody pulp.

After one incident, which Ben won but which left him with a broken rib, split knuckles and two black eyes, the owner gave him a gun and paid for time at a range so that he could learn how to use it.

Ben had an affinity for guns. Great aim, which improved with practice, an eye that seemed perfect even if the scope was off. He knew the damage a gun could do—saw it up close and personal one night—and vowed never to use one except in self-defense.

Of course, self-defense isn't always what the cops make it out to be.

Ben had been on a delivery when the owner's supplier went to the club and took it down. Ben may have been passing on the funds, but the owner hadn't been. The club burned with only employees inside, the result, the cops said, of free-basing, matches and too much alcohol. Everyone died. The warning was sent—and the only person left to get it was Ben.

As he saw it, he had three choices: run for the rest of his life, beg for the supplier's (nonexistent) mercy, or defend himself. He defended himself with a coldness he hadn't realized he had. He planned the attack as calmly as he planned anything, knowing that he could simply be firing the first volley in a war that would never end.

But warnings could be sent both ways, and he wanted the community to know that no one fucked with him. He cashed everything out, moved out of his apartment, and became a ghost.

Six months of work, tracking connections, finding people who specialized in being lost, and then taking care of them, quickly, efficiently, and with a minimum of fuss.

He was nearly done when they caught him. Lost five guys taking him down, wounding him badly enough that he could no longer defend himself.

That was when he learned he hadn't prepared enough. The club owner had been a small fish, the supplier another small fish, the people he took out more small fish. The man who talked to him was probably a medium fish, one who claimed to represent a larger fish.

He offered Ben training for a job, a high-paying one that he'd have to work only a few times a year.

"You have an affinity for it," the medium fish said. "Shame to let such talent go to waste."

He never wasted it. Somewhere, he lost Ben, the boy bouncer, and became the ghost, the man who could go from place to place and never be recognized, the man who had fifteen layers between himself and the world.

***

YEARS LATER, when Glenna saw that incident in his chart, she said, "You lost everything and it stripped you down to your warrior nature. Since then, you've never looked back."

He sees no point in looking back. He learns his lesson and moves forward, in the world and not a part of it.

Losing everything means only one thing now: losing himself.

***

THE AFTERNOON SUN is pale through the smog. Cars honk, tourists gawk at the poverty that is Hollywood Boulevard, and he remembers why he hates Los Angeles.

He didn't expect such news. He has been careless in recent months—having his own chart done only when he had a job. May was, literally, uncharted territory.

Until now.

He pulls the cell phone out of its pouch on his belt. This phone is one he cloned in Detroit a week ago. He hasn't used it yet, so it's as clean as the phone in his rental and the five he stashed at the airport.

As he walks, he dials. Glenna will be able to explain this chart. She'll run it herself and tell him what the darkness is, what the nothing is. She isn't afraid of him, and she has the experience to understand every nuance a chart can make.

He listens to the rings as he passes a diner filled with transvestites, hookers, and wannabe stars. His rental is parked halfway up the next road, around a curve, up a hill, impossible to see from the main thoroughfare.

Even when he hasn't agreed to a job, he's cautious.

"Cosmos," says an unfamiliar male voice, loud through the earpiece.

No "May I Help You?," no "Leading the Way in Harmony," which is the store's tagline, something Glenna always insists her employees say. In fact, this man's voice is so flat he sounds disinterested, like a cop who is answering the phone to see who is on the other end.

Still, he decides to play it, just to see. "Glenna, please."

"Who's calling?"

"I need a name, sir," and he knows his hunch is right. Glenna has never screened her calls. Not in the ten years he's known her.

A person has to take what comes, she says, *however it comes.*

She is, if he remembers right, some combination of Pisces, Cancer and Aquarius, all intuition and emotion, sensitive, psychic and unique. Certainly not someone who would respond well to a voice as cold as this one.

He decides to push one last time. "Glenna has never asked for my name before. Just put her on."

"No can do, sir," the voice says. "I need a name."

He hangs up, then shuts off the phone, slipping it into his pocket. He'll toss it when he gets onto the freeway, somewhere near a bridge or an off-ramp near gang territory. After he wipes it down, of course.

It isn't until he gets to his rental that he realizes he's shaken. It's such an unfamiliar emotion, he's forgotten how it feels—the chill down the back, the twisting in the stomach, the unsteady nerves in the hand.

For he was wrong when he thought the only thing he had left was himself. He has Glenna, his seer, his touchstone, and the only person he's trusted since he started down this road twenty years before.

***

THE WEB IS an anonymous man's the best friend. On it, he has found sites that have told him how to pick hotel keycard locks, how to buy illegal and untraceable weapons, how to steal identities.

Now, in the privacy of his touristy hotel near Universal Studios, he uses the Web to learn something he does not want to know.

Glenna is dead.

Not just dead. Murdered. Two days before, in what the Flagstaff newspaper is calling a gangland style hit. In other words, a professional job.

He gets more information from the local radio news sites and a Phoenix newspaper that feels an obligation to cover the entire state. The details are familiar. He recognizes the method. The job was a quickie, gun left on the scene registered to a New Orleans police detective who had it stolen (or in New Orleans, with its corrupt department, who sold it) at a take-down five years ago. Hit happened late at night, in a private corner near a vegan restaurant she frequented. One shot, taken no more than three feet away, and not heard by the locals. Silencer, probably, or pillow or purse to muffle the sound.

There were probably other details the cops were keeping to themselves, things like a stranger seen near the store that day or that night, an abandoned rental car, wiped clean, or evidence pointing to a local, evidence that didn't pan out.

The thing that disturbs him the most is that the local police don't handle it themselves. They don't even call Phoenix for help. They assume it is a hit, which means the gunman has organized connections, and they call in the FBI.

He's glad now that the cloned phone is gone. He needs to be gone too. No time to delay. There's probably someone tracking his steps in Hollywood as he's closing his laptop.

Check out is easy. Tourist hotels, gotta love 'em. The staff doesn't care why he's leaving early. They figure they know. Too much fun in the sun. Too many rides. Too much alcohol, not enough money.

He slips out as quietly as he slipped in, drops the rental at LAX, and hops the next Southwest flight to Vegas.

For the first time in years, he needs real help, and there's only one place he can get it.

***

HE FLIES SOUTHWEST because they let customers pick their own seats. If you don't like who you sit next to, you can move, no questions asked. He takes a window toward the back, grabs an airsick bag, and makes himself look queasy.

No one sits next to him.

The short flight is uneventful, but his mind is racing. Glenna may have mob connections, but he doubts it. She may have an ex-husband with access, but he doesn't believe that. Hell, she may be the mother of a high school cheerleader whose jealous rival hires a hit man, but he never believed that story in the first place. He certainly doesn't believe it now.

He has a hunch he's her only connection to the dark world he lives in.

Should I be afraid for myself, old friend? My chart was uncertain. It told me that today would introduce me to Death.

He leans against the tiny window, staring at the tops of clouds. She had told him at that first reading that charts weren't easily predictable. She'd looked at his and thought that he was a stand-in for Death because of his job.

I did meet Death yesterday, just not in the way I thought.

She had been wrong twice. Her chart had said that day would introduce her to Death. Without him, Death would never have found her, at least not in this way.

He doesn't need actual proof. He has more important things to worry about.

He needs to figure out if she's a warning or if she's a tool. Or both. The shooter had to know the cops would find her long before he did. If the shooter were after him and knew about Glenna, all the shooter had to do was wait.

So he's not an obvious target. He's something else, but what he doesn't know.

She had his charts for the next job. His chart, the client's chart, and the victim's chart. No names, only reference numbers. Numbers she promised—and he checked (late one night, easily breaking into that silly little store)—that never had names attached to them.

She never had his real name anyway or his address. He always contacted her, and she didn't seem to mind.

All she had was birthdates, times, and locations.

That was plenty.

His right hand crumples the airsick bag. He is still shaken, and beneath that feeling is something else, something even more unsettling.

He does not want to examine what that feeling is.

**

ANGEL BRIDGES has an astrology palace near one of the Elvis chapels on the strip. The astrology palace is as garish as anything else in Vegas: six stories high with turrets and neon astrological symbols that flash on and off depending on the time of year and the fluctuations in the cosmos.

Angel makes her money telling gamblers how to bet based on the stars, but she runs a side business for true believers. She makes no money on that one—she does it strictly for love. And she never asks questions because she values her life and her position in a town where people do anything to guarantee luck.

It's five o'clock when he walks in, the beginning of her evening rush. One of the little waifs who works as an assistant approaches him, but he ignores it. The waif bleats, but he continues to walk toward Angel, cutting ahead of a long and patient line.

She sits on a thick couch, a caftan spread around her ample frame. Diamonds glitter on her ears and fingers— she can't lead other people to wealth if it doesn't look like she has some of her own.

She sees him, smiles at her current customer, and excuses herself, as if she's going to get more research material. She disappears behind a gold leaf door. He takes a side hallway that seems to go in the opposite direction, but doesn't.

They end up in her office, an ergonomically correct room with no windows and a skylight that, at night, sends patterns of neon across the darkened floor. He learned that at one a.m. on a Christmas Eve as he checked her files, making sure her connections were clean ones.

As she closes the metal door, he hands her the natal chart. She's never seen it before. She's only done client charts for him. She has no idea it's his.

"I need two months," he says, "starting with April 20th of this year. And I'm going to wait for it."

He's never done that before. He's always come back. She peers at him, then adjusts her red wig. He doesn't like it. She looks better with her natural black.

"It's gonna cost," she says. "I'll lose about a quarter of the suckers out there."

"I'll pay," he says.

She nods, presses a button, and tells an assistant to inform the clients she's received news of a change in the stars. Then she focuses on the chart and punches up something on her computer.

He takes an upholstered chair designed for a frame shorter and heavier than his. It's the most uncomfortable chair he's ever sat in. But he doesn't move. Instead, he ponders.

A hit like that always draws the FBI, later rather than sooner in small towns, although he probably should expect sophistication in a strange little town like Sedona. What will the FBI learn from his files?

Too much, actually, if they plug the dates, place names, and birth times into their unsolved data base. One half of the birth information will tie to hits all over the country. It won't take a rocket scientist to figure out that the other half belong to the folks who paid good money to get the first half out of the way.

And then there's his, of course, and its repeated monthly or weekly charts. Not that it'll do the Feds much good. Ben disappeared twenty years ago. A ghost took his place, a ghost no one has been able to trace for a very long time.

They will get his patterns though and, if they put someone smart on the case, a pretty good analysis of his MO, damn his perfectionist Virgo side. They'll also get an excellent description of him from neighboring shop-keepers and former employees because they'll know what questions to ask.

And from the client list, they'll probably track down a few of his hackers or maybe the fronts who took the order. His carefully formed fifteen will crumble to six or seven or four.

One piece of information and his operation shatters. Was that the goal? Or is he being neutralized because the big fish is finally gone or because someone has finally caught up with him?

They'd caught up with him before, but always failed in hand-to-hand. It took some planning to make him ineffective. Some planning and some unwitting compliance from himself and his superstitions.

He'd gotten complacent, a bad thing in his business.

"This is a piece of shit chart," Angel says.

"Inaccurate?" he asks.

"No, just incomplete, like they were using one of those computer downloads done by someone who only gives half a crap." She runs a bejeweled hand over her eyes. What is it about these astrologers that makes them wear too much jewelry on their fingers?

"So whatever this person told me is incomplete?"

"Dunno," Angel says. "What'd you get told?"

He slips the other chart to her, the one with the week ahead.

Angel frowns at it. "Why're you going to a crap artist when you got me?"

"You're not always with me, babe," he says, folding his hands together and leaning back.

She shakes her head, then she pushes the weekly sheet to him. "Look at this. It doesn't tie. It's as if this astrologer's forgotten the natal chart. We got a birthdate in Eastern Standard Time, and we got an analysis done for someone born in Western Daylight. Doesn't work. This is so basic."

"So it's wrong," he says.

"This weekly thing is a piece of garbage." She tosses it into the nearby wastebasket with a flourish. "But this natal chart, I gotta tell you, is the nastiest thing I've ever seen."

"Because of how it's done?"

"Because of what it means." She frowns at him, shoves the wig back so far he can see the pink of her scalp. "This is another client?"

He nods, not trusting himself to answer.

"This is one mean s.o.b. Dangerous. He thinks he's clean, but he's not. He kills for a living, and even though charts can be figurative, I don't think this one is. He sees himself as a warrior, but he's an assassin, plain and simple. Not the kind of person nice folks should hang with."

He hasn't moved, his hands still across his stomach, his feet stretched out, his body trapped in the world's most uncomfortable chair. But his muscles have all gone tense. He can feel the gun beneath his suit coat. He hopes his expression hasn't changed, then he wonders if it should have changed. After all, she's just told him one of his clients is a killer.

"What're you supposed to do for this guy?" she asks, and he mentally curses her, wishing that she would remember she's not supposed to ask questions. "A job, like the others?"

He nods.

"I hope it's a legal job. You don't want to mess with this guy in any real way."

"What else does the natal chart tell you?" he asks. Somehow his voice remains calm.

"That he's got more secrets than God. That he's unpredictable and charming and could turn on you in a second. I won't do anything for him, no matter how much he paid me."

She's trying to be nice to him. She doesn't know. His muscles are freezing up. He's holding back the truth, that she has worked for him for five years, thinks he's a friend, thinks he's someone she can trust.

"Well," he says, "let's see what the two-month chart says."

"You don't seem shocked by this."

"I thought he was shady. You're not surprising me."

She nods, focuses on the computer screen. For a long time, all he hears is the tap-tap of keys. He resists the urge to stand and pace.

They had to have already found some of his people. The only way to get to Glenna was to find out about the blind box in Flagstaff. In the past, he used to go there, pick up the stuff and drive it down. Three years ago, he decided she could open the box on occasion. He brought her a key, and sometimes he would call, asking her to pick up the various charts. She would.

A few of his hackers and a couple of his fronts have that address. Others have a blind box in Vegas and another in L.A. If the cops triangulated that cell phone call, they know he was in L.A. Or maybe someone else knows.

He gets up so abruptly the chair bangs against the floor. Angel starts. "You okay?"

"Need to make a private call," he says. "I'll be right back."

"Take your time," she says. "This is one confusing mass of planets."

He doesn't like that sound either. He heads to the door, takes the corridor outside and goes in the Elvis chapel. There's a line here too, mostly of drunks. He congratulates one of the champagne drinking men, lifts his cell as he pats him on the side, and then goes onto the strip.

It's changed over the years. Big buildings loom over him, pretending to be something they aren't—the Eiffel Tower, the Empire State Building, a complete European City State. The neon lights make it as bright as day. Cars pass, people stumble by, many of them holding buckets with tokens in them or nickels. A few have newspapers and others clutch cash as if it isn't real.

He dials the store in L.A., hoping it's open late. On the fifth ring, a woman answers. He recognizes the voice. The palm reader.

"You get Elli May out of there," he says.

"So it's you." The reader curses him in some romance language—probably Italian. "You could have warned her."

"I had no idea."

"She comes here looking for adventure, not a gun in the face."

A gun in the face? He hadn't expected that. He expected something a few days away, maybe an FBI visit or a discreet contact. Not a direct attack. "Is she all right?"

"Scared. She gave him all her charts. He didn't want money. A good thing, eh? So now she can go back to those parents of hers, the ones who didn't even care that she was gone." The reader curses him again.

He lets her. "Who put the gun in her face?"

"I don't know his name."

"Have you seen him before?"

"No," she says.

"What can you tell me about him?"

"Why should I tell you anything?"

"Because I may be able to prevent him from coming back."

She pauses. He can feel her brain whirling. He wonders if he's making a mistake, calling her, if the attacker is still there. Then he decides it doesn't matter. Most folks can't track a cell phone call. Even if she has Caller I.D., all she can find out is what the cell phone number is, not where the call originates.

"He came in about three hours ago," she says. "He was young, white, has money—or at least thinks he does. Hand-tailored suit, but dirty shoes, like he's been traveling or forgets to shine them."

He listens, body tense.

"He points the gun at me first, and I shrug. I've seen guns before, but not eyes like his. Big and brown and spinning, almost. Crazy. He thinks he's smart, but he's only smart like a fox. This kind does not survive long."

Is she talking to the attacker now? Or is this the kind of way she always speaks? He wishes he had paid more attention to her, instead of dismissing her out of hand.

"He wants the charts. He gets angry when he finds out they're all the same birthdate. He wants the other ones, the client charts. She says she has no idea what he means, but she gives him everything. He slaps the gun across her face and she falls. I've got my own gun and I pull it out. He turns, laughs at me, says, 'Grandma, you're no match for me,' and then he leaves, as if the fact we seen him don't matter, as if his visit is normal."

"Then what?" he asks.

"A call to the police, of course. No one's come yet. This part of town, who cares? But you care. You know this man."

"No," he says. "I don't."

"He knows you. He says you're getting old and tired and you don't even realize it. A relic, he calls you. A superstitious relic." She pauses. "You will not come back here."

"That's right."

"I am telling you, you will not come back here. My niece, she thinks he will murder you. She thinks it is her fault."

"Tell her that her chart is off. She forgot to adjust for time zones." And he hangs up.

He wipes the phone off and then tosses it on the sidewalk outside the Elvis chapel. The drunk will think it has fallen from its perch in his pocket. It won't be until he gets his bill that he realizes something has gone wrong.

He goes back into the astrology palace. The line is shorter. The person who was having his chart done still waiting near the couch, only now he is checking his watch.

He slips into the back, goes to the office. She has swiveled her chair so that she's working on a back desk, using protractors and paper charts and colored pencils. It takes him a moment to realize she's redoing her work by hand.

"What's the problem?" he asks.

"It comes out the same," she says and she sounds complete surprised. "Even with the proper adjustments, this weekly chart comes out exactly the same. Something started a week ago, something very serious, which led to a great loss a few days ago, one which had an impact today."

At that, she looks up at him, as if he can give her the information she seeks. He can, of course, but he won't.

When it becomes clear that he'll say nothing, she continues. "It builds and then there is nothing."

"Nothing?" he asks, beginning to hate that word. "What the hell is nothing?"

She shrugs. "I've never seen anything like it. There is no more chart."

"So it means death."

She shakes her head. "I've seen death in charts before, often charts you give me, sometimes in the gamblers' charts. But it usually appears as a transformation. A person's life continues even if he does not."

"What the hell does that mean?"

She smiles. This is clearly a conversation she's familiar with. "Let's say you die tomorrow. Your financial affairs will continue. Your relationships will continue, at least for a little while. You may still have an impact on the world, long after you're gone. I suppose eventually the chart will come to nothing, but I have never seen one do that. Usually the person who dies does not come back for another reading."

That last she says wryly, as if humor might help her unease. It doesn't help his.

If he stops, if he ends, nothing will continue. He has no relationships, not like she is talking about. He has no friends and family (well, he has a family, but they are not people he has thought of in decades. He left them when he stopped being Ben, maybe even before, when he went to work in the City), and his finance affairs will become untended accounts that banks all over the world will have to deal with some day.

He has no will, no legacy, no real life. When he goes, he will leave nothing behind. He will evaporate, like a spirit in the wind.

"I don't understand," he says.

"Neither do I," she says and frowns. "All we have is a cataclysmic event and then nothing. Perhaps I should run my own chart. Perhaps the world is going to end."

She does not say this with humor. He stares at her, then he flings five times her usual payment on the desk. "Thanks."

"Come back tomorrow," she says. "I'll research this, see if anyone else knows what it means."

"I think you might just want to let this go," he says. "I am."

"I can't let it go. It may have great meaning."

"I doubt it," he says, and lets himself out the door.

The line is even shorter. The man waiting for his reading is talking angrily to one of the waifs.

He goes outside, looks at the fake towns, the people pretending they're having a good time. The cell phone is gone from the sidewalk in front of the Elvis chapel. He wonders if the drunk found it or if someone else picked it up.

It is time to disappear. To become a true ghost, never thought or heard of again. Over the years, he has made a hundred escape plans, and he has liked none of them. Nothing sounds duller than sitting on a tropical beach sipping Mai Tais for the rest of his life.

No matter what Angel said, or how much contempt she said it with, he *is* a warrior. And he wants to die a warrior's death. If he cannot work, he cannot enjoy his life.

Maybe he should cut all his ties with the past, the fifteen layers (some of which are gone, some of which have betrayed him), move to a different country, and set up again. Someday, perhaps, he can come back here as an independent and start again.

But he is too old to start again. He only has ten more good years, twenty if he keeps himself in perfect condition and chooses targets as old or older than he is.

Perhaps the nothing on his chart reflects his ghost status. Perhaps it means that he will choose a new identity, with a new birthdate, and start again.

Perhaps. But he does not believe it. He has reached the end, and he is not sure what that means.

But he knows what he will do.

He will wait.

∗∗∗

WHAT HE FIGURES IS THIS:

The young man is after him for his client list, which means he has not found the fronts, only the hackers. In fact, he may have only found one hacker—any one with Flagstaff PO Box would do.

What disturbs him is the connection to astrology. The guy knew about the superstition somehow—and he thinks he knows how. Sometimes hit men become legends in their own business, especially if they've been around a while, like he has. They get monikers, usually based on something unusual.

He hasn't been tied into the network in years—too much risk, risk he doesn't like. But the network is still tied to him, clearly, or to his reputation. They can't call him the Zodiac Killer—that had been taken by some psycho who wouldn't know a pro hit if he were instructed in how to do one—so they probably gave him a different name: the Horoscope Man, the Astrology Hits, something. And from there, this guy searched until he found something unusual.

What doesn't fit, what bothers him, is that the guy's research makes him seem cautious, but his encounters—both with Glenna and Elli May—make him seem like a quickie.

The guy's also arrogant, so he doesn't cover his tracks. The fact that he has the charts is both exhilarating and disturbing. Disturbing because the guy's going to get caught and he's going to give up what he knows. Exhilarating, because the FBI, even though they're involved, don't have the charts and can't tie Glenna's clients to anything.

If the guy is as smart as he seems, he's going to find out about Vegas. Once he finds Vegas, he'll find Angel. Once he finds Angel, his spree will end, one way or another.

There's even a timetable, according to the weekly chart. By the sixth of May, the guy'll be in Vegas—and there'll be a confrontation. Better to know that in advance. No surprises.

No surprises, the better the chance of winning.

If there is something to win.

***

WHAT HE DOESN'T ADMIT to himself as he waits is how disturbed he is. Deep down. He's never been anyone's focus, never been the source of anyone's search—not him, not his ghostly self. Sure, he's probably in a bunch of police and FBI databases, but for his various crimes.

Right now, he's being tailed for who he is, targeted for what he knows, and the people he's surrounded himself with are being punished.

He hates that.

He hasn't realized how much he hates that until he sits in Angel's office for the second night in a row, trying to find a comfortable chair. The lights are out, but the skylight lets in so much neon ambiance that everything is well lit.

The computer is off, but he has helped himself to her files, realizes she has some connections that make him nervous. He wonders if they know who he is, if they know about his previous break-in, and if they care.

Probably not. If they cared, they'd take care of him. They're probably watching now, just to see what he's doing, just to find out what he knows.

What he knows is that he's having a hard time staying calm. And that's not like him. But he keeps thinking of Glenna, her easy manner, her smile when she saw him after a long absence, the way she believed whatever she did was for the best.

He led the guy right to her, and she had died, violently, because of him.

Strangely enough, that disturbs him. When he gets paid to take a life, that's different. It isn't about him. It's what he does. It's not personal.

This is. This loss had a direct connection to him, more direct than pulling the trigger.

This loss pisses him off. And the fact that it pisses him off pisses him off even more. He isn't supposed to have attachments. He's outgrown them. They're useless in his business. He needs to be a complete loner, and somehow he's failed to do that.

Part of him worried about Angel until he saw who she was dealing with. If the guy offs her, he'll have an entire family of people to answer to. She'll be protected.

It's his remaining astrologers who are in trouble. Them, and his hackers—the ones who haven't encountered the guy—and the fronts, and all the others associated with this little operation. He's struggled to keep them as clean as possible. He doesn't want anything to happen to them because of him.

At least, that's what he's telling himself as he sits in the shadows, watching the blue neon Scorpio signal—an M with a pointed tail—flash on and off against the cherry colored carpet. He's also thinking he may have overestimated this guy when he hears the security lock click open.

Finally.

He pulls out the semi he got at a militia convention outside of Denver and aims it at the door. He has to wait until he's sure because he doesn't want to nail Angel by mistake.

Someone slips inside, as thin as one of the waifs. The neon is off for the moment, dammit, and the room is darker than usual. Then the gold Taurus ignites—a circle with horns—and he sees the leather jacket, the slicked-back hair, the cruel curve to the mouth.

"You could've just asked for my client list," he says.

The guy swivels, surprised. But he covers well. "I had to find you first."

His answer is a spray of bullets that rip the guy up and make him dance before slumping against the wall, lifeless and empty.

Now he's got to move quick. He suspects the palace has walls thick enough to hide the noise, but suspecting is not the same as knowing. He approaches the body, gaping and bloody where the torso should be, and stares at the face.

Unfamiliar, not that he should know who the guy was. And young, arrogant. A quickie, just like he thought. He slips on his gloves and pats the pockets, finding a Hilton room key and a receipt with the room number, and a wallet with I.D. poorly faked, from some computer site.

Not even a quickie then. An amateur, a wannabe. No wonder he needed the client list. He didn't have connections to get jobs on his own. Glenna had been practice, proof that he could do it.

And maybe he couldn't. A real pro would've shot Elli May and the palm reader. A real pro wouldn't've left such an obvious trail.

A tiny red light is blinking on the back of the computer. He looks for the source—thinking maybe someone has a laser scope on him. How can that be? There's no way to focus the scope on him from that angle. There should be shadows from the skylight above. He's been checking. The astrological signs are sending the proper light to the carpet.

Some kind of warning light. Some kind of security trigger. He pockets the room key, but destroys the receipt. Then he peels off his gloves, and folds them over his shoes like a cheap pair of rubbers. There'll be bloody footprints. He can't help that. But that's the only clue they'll have, and with Angel's unsavory connections, the cops'll probably look somewhere else.

He reaches for the door, turns the knob, hears a second click. Not a security lock this time. Something flat and ominous, something he should have expected, but didn't because this, for him, was a quickie too.

He pulls on the door, but it doesn't open. Programmed to lock after violence like that. He's seen security like this before. He's not going to be able to shoot through the metal door, at least not in time.

"Damn," he says as he turns, hoping he has time to get up to the skylight, to break through it. The red light on the computer is blinking so fast that it seems almost constant.

He stands on one of the uncomfortable chairs, the semi pointed at the skylight. He's pulling the trigger when the computer explodes.

***

He has time to analyze it.

It's not really a white light. It's more like sunlight, broad and glistening, incorporating many colors, but so brightly that all he can see is white.

He's afraid to look at it, afraid he'll see that no one is waiting for him, or that the folks who are waiting are really, really, really pissed off.

He hides his eyes, but the light comes through the lids, just like it would do if he were really there. He doesn't look at it, pretends he can't feel its warm glow, and gradually, it fades away as if it never existed.

As if he never existed.

Which, he supposes, he hasn't, not for a very long time.

***

"Ben?"

He opens his eyes. The old lady standing over him has thin gray hair and a broad face. Her features are familiar.

"Ben?" She sounds like she's witnessing a miracle. Behind her head, a TV screen blares the news. A woman is reading headlines, and below her is a sports ticker. It gives the score of the All-Star game.

He frowns. The old lady is calling for nurses, and he realizes that he's in a bed, immobile, and very, very tired.

"You're back, Ben. Thank God. I've been here everyday."

Finally he recognizes the voice. The old lady is Angel. He was wrong. Her hair's natural color isn't black. The tips are, but she's stopped dying it. A scarf lays on an end table, along with a book about destiny. She's been waiting for him, and reading.

"You saved my life. That serial killer—"

She doesn't get a chance to finish. His room is invaded by scores of health care professionals in white coats. They surround him, stick him with things, ask him questions he doesn't know the answer to, tell him he's lucky, lucky, lucky to be alive.

He has lost more than two months. It's mid-July. He has been immobile in a Vegas hospital bed for two months—not alive, not dead.

Living in limbo. Existing. He was, he realizes, during that span, nothing at all.

They take Angel out, afraid she'll tire him, but she promises to come back.

He has to cope with many realizations—that his rehabilitation will take months, maybe years. He may not walk again. His left arm has been destroyed. He's afraid to look at his face.

They found out his real identity from his fingerprints, sent for his family, and found out he has none left. His fingerprints are on file, he remembers, because of a drug bust twenty years ago, one the club owner paid their way out of. He had forgotten that. He has forgotten more than he knows.

What he does learn from Angel over the next few days is that, in her eyes, he's a hero. Somehow, she thinks, he got the guy's chart. They're calling the guy—Dante Evans—a serial killer who specialized in astrologers.

Evans wasn't as careful as he thought. He left clues at the scene of Glenna's murder and Elli May was able to I.D. him from a photo as the guy who beat her the afternoon of May fourth.

Angel believes that "Ben" knew something was wrong, and when he figured it out, guarded her. She has no clue who he really is, and if she has no clue, then neither do her contacts—the ones who booby-trapped her office.

She is embarrassed as she explains this. "They made me promise that I'd keep their information secure," she says. "They set up this trap. At first it was supposed to go off if there was unofficial activity in the room, but I was afraid for my assistants, so they set it up to go off if there was other factors. I never asked what those factors were. They promised it would never happen."

He knows. It could have been any number of things: a response to the cordite, to the sound of gunfire, to the spray of warm liquid—like blood. Or merely a remote device, set off by someone who kept an eye on the place, whenever he believed there was trouble.

Gunfire counted as trouble.

But he says nothing to her, and he also says nothing when she offers to pay for his room. His tracks are covered, so deep that he knows he's facing an opportunity.

Angel sits beside his bed. She's still apologizing to him, feeling guilty for misreading the chart. She doesn't understand that it's not Evans' chart, that it's his chart, but he won't tell her that.

"I still have trouble believing death registers as nothing. But they can't find anything about him. We're the only ones affected," she says.

He listens. He doesn't tell her what he believes. Can't. He's afraid she'll run his chart or the serial killer's chart, which is what she believes it is. If she runs it past May 11, she'll find the nothing ended on the day he woke up. The nothing was the coma.

Even though it wasn't really nothing, not like the chart said. After all, Angel's here and she thinks he's a hero. He has had some impact on her life.

Maybe the nothing was a misinterpretation—or a non-interpretation. Maybe everything was in such flux that no one could predict what would happen.

"Angel," he says, when she finally pauses for breath, "do you believe in second chances?"

"Of course, honey," she says and pats his good hand. "The religions, they all deal with that. It's even in a person's chart, in the nodes. Past lives always have an impact on present ones."

"No, no," he says. "I'm talking about this life. What if there's a clear line, a break between what you were before and now. Can you be something else?"

She studies him for a moment. He wonders how clearly she's seeing him. Does she think he's talking about his old drug arrest, his wandering lifestyle? Or does she think something deeper is going on, maybe even suspect the darkness he let take over his soul?

"I think a person gets a second chance like that for a reason," she says, "and only a fool would pass it by."

He nods. He's been thinking that too.

"You want me to do your chart, so we can see what path you should walk?"

"No," he says. He's done with that. Charts are too accurate. He's not going to plan his life like that any more. Besides, he wants to forget that he's a warrior with a judge's soul. He wants to think he's been reborn in July. A Cancer. Sensitive, nurturing, protective. Someone else entirely.

"How come you never told me who you really are, Ben?" she asks, looking down. This question matters to her.

He gives it due consideration. "I guess," he says, "because I never knew myself."

Protected by fifteen layers, a soldier in a war he didn't believe in or understand, searching for meaning where there was none, meaning that got the wrong people killed.

He's not a hero, not even close. Doubts he ever can be. He's still superstitious, maybe more so than he was before. He's hanging up his weapons and finding a new path—one that might make him worthy of the light.

Maybe, the next time it surrounds him, he can look at it and through it, to the world beyond. Maybe the next time, he'll have enough courage to go there, and face himself, what he's been and what he's done.

The thought disturbs him and he closes his eyes, for the first time in his own memory not trying to repress feeling, but to acknowledge it.

To feel something where there was once nothing.

To be a person instead of a ghost.

Stomping Mad

SHE CALLED HERSELF the Martha Stewart of Science Fiction, and she looked the part: Homecoming-queen pretty with a touch of maliciousness behind the eyes, a fakely tolerant acceptance of everyone fannish, and an ability to throw the best room party at any given Worldcon in any given year.

So when a body was found in her party suite, the case came to me. Folks in fandom call me the Sam Spade of Science Fiction, but I'm actually more like the Nero Wolfe: a man who prefers good food and good conversation, a man who is huge, both in his appetite and in his education. I don't go out much, except to science fiction conventions (a world in and of themselves) and to dinner with the rare comrade. I surround myself with books, computers, and televisions. I do not have orchids or an Archie Goodwin, but I do possess a sharp eye for detail and a critical understanding of the dark side of human nature.

I have, in the past, solved over a dozen cases, ranging from finding the source of a doomsday virus that threatened to shut down the world's largest fan database to discovering who had stolen the Best Artist Hugo two hours before the award ceremony. My reputation had grown during the last British Fantasy Convention when I—an American—worked with Scotland Yard to recover a diamond worth £1,000,000 that a Big Name Fan had forgotten to put in the hotel's safe.

But I had never faced a more convoluted criminal mind until that Friday afternoon at the First Annual Jurassic Parkathon, a media convention held in Anaheim.

**

THE CONVENTION WAS OFFICIALLY called Dinocon I because Crichton's people, or Spielberg's people, or some studio's people wouldn't give permission to use the Jurassic Park name with a non-sanctioned project. I normally don't get involved with a media con, especially one held in Anaheim, but this one had a million dollar budget and a state-of-the-art computer system, and I simply couldn't resist the challenge.

So I was in Ops with most of the folks running the con when the call came through. Ops, for those of you who've never seen one, is a hotel function room with most of the furniture removed, replaced with tables covered with computer equipment, too many chairs, and tons of print out paper. Most of the people working Ops look haggard and stressed by the time the convention starts, and many of them are ready to collapse by the time it's over. So we really didn't need to hear some security person, young by the sound of him, on the two-way radio:

"Hey, ah, we got a, um, Situation X, here."

Everyone in Ops snapped to attention. The actual term was a File X—always a pun, everything a pun—and it was only supposed to be used for an extreme emergency.

"Copy that," Doris, a muscular woman the size of Stallone, said. She headed security, and had at every major con I'd ever worked on. Security is important at sf conventions, perhaps *the* most important thing, because these cons, as most of you know, aren't your simple suit-tie-and-briefcase affairs. The big conventions have three levels: the fans, most of whom dress in costume (some medieval barbarians, some Captain Kirk, some space aliens); the pros, most of whom write, act, or somehow work in the science fiction field; the dealers, most of whom sell sf paraphernalia—books, videos, posters, and the ubiquitous Bajoran earrings. Media cons had more earrings, videos, and actors; fewer books, writers, and intellectual discussions. Behind it all is the con-com, the army of people who run the entire shebang, and put out any and all fires along the way. Security deals with most of those: from regular hotel guests who are scared by the werewolf in the elevator to the teenagers who've stayed up all night playing the card game *Magic*, and who suddenly think it fun to pull the fire alarm on the second floor.

Never, in my twenty years of fandom, have we gotten a call for this kind emergency, and never have I heard a security person sound so scared.

"It's in room 4708. Can someone come here?" The security kid's voice cracked, confirming my suspicion: he was a volunteer, and he was eighteen at most.

"What's the nature of the emergency?" Doris asked.

"I don't think you want me to describe it on an open channel," the kid said.

"All right, be right there," Doris said, and left.

We mused about the "Situation" X for a moment. "Maybe," Ruth, the con chair, said, "he saw a fur bikini for the first time."

"It's the masquerade tonight," John said behind her, and we all laughed. He probably saw a costume, got scared, and decided to call it in. We'd all had that happen before.

"Or maybe it's pea soup," said Ben, and I, being most senior on the staff, groaned. I remembered that one, which had now eased into fannish legend. Just after *The Exorcist* came out, some fans in Baltimore held a room party and served pea soup along with the usual potato chips, cheese, and beer. After midnight, when the crowd got really drunk, someone had the brilliant idea of imitating Linda Blair in the famous vomit sequence. Of course, everyone had to do it, and by the time security arrived, a sea of pea soup was running down the corridor like the Blob without the assistance of the special effects people.

"Please, ghod, anything but that," I said.

At that moment, the phone rang. Ruth answered, and handed it to me, her tired face filled with confusion and surprise. "It's Doris," she said. "For you."

I slid my chair back and grabbed the phone, feeling as confused as Ruth looked. Doris could have radioed me. That would have been procedure. Maybe something was really up in 4708.

"Yeah?" I said.

"Spade," she said—my fannish friends had called me Spade since I solved the first case almost twelve years before—"you've gotta come up here. Now."

"What's going on?" I asked.

"An absolute disaster," she said, and hung up.

"Why didn't she use the radio?" Ruth asked.

I shrugged. "I guess she didn't want anyone else wandering up to the room." I eased myself out of my special chair, the one that I insist a con-com bring to every convention if they want my services, and with a push of a button, shut down the financial files on Dinocon's main computer. Then I made my way slowly—because I never hurry—to the fourth floor of the main convention hotel.

Dinocon had 8,000 registered attendees, and it was only Friday afternoon. The convention was scheduled to go through Sunday, and another 2,000 people were expected at the door on Saturday. Most of these folks were already crowding the halls, having conversations with friends they hadn't seen for a while and trying to discover where that night's parties would be held. I squeezed my way through—negotiating packed hallways was never easy for a man of my bulk—and made it to the elevator in time to nab the last spot. No one complained, though, as I squooshed people toward the back. Part of that was my con-com badge—regular con attendees knew better than to harass a person in a con-com badge—and part of it was my reputation.

"Hey, Spade!" someone yelled from the back. "You get a piece of that diamond?"

"I don't charge for my services," I said, in a gently chiding voice. I made my money years ago as an early employee of Microsoft. I took all my bonuses in stock, and then retired at the age of 31, not as rich as Bill Gates, but rich enough.

"He's a gentleman detective," someone else said from the back, and the entire elevator chuckled.

"Imagine," I said as the doors opened on four, "a gentleman—and a scholar."

I got off, but not before I heard more giggling as the doors closed. Fannish humor was not the stuff of stand-up routines, but it was usually full of sweet, if not always socially adept, affection.

The room 4708 was on what had been designated by the hotel as a party floor. On these floors, it was okay to have loud conversation all night, to serve beer in rooms, and to talk in the hallways. Other floors, the non-party floors, were for people who actually wanted to sleep during the con, something I hadn't done in the last thirteen conventions I had attended.

Photocopied 8"x11" signs were taped onto the wallpaper, most of them announcing bid parties for other conventions. The signs on 4708 looked professionally done on slick glossy paper. They announced the first annual Literature Con to be held in an ancient Hilton an hour outside of Manhattan. I stared at the signs for a moment, frowning. Anyone with half a brain knew that most of Dinocon's attendees weren't likely to attend a literature con, especially one held all the way across the country. But the posters had another draw besides their slick appearance.

Food.

Come to our bid party, the sign read, *and dine at your heart's content. Award-winning chocolates, Lucinda's World Famous Chili, and gourmet dishes from the farthest reaches of the Solar System. Come to* the *party of the convention. You'll talk about it for the next three lifetimes.*

Curiouser and curiouser. Lucinda was Lucinda Danielle Stanhope, also known as the Martha Stewart of Science Fiction. Lucinda hated media cons, thinking that they ruined "pure" science fiction. Pure science fiction, to her, was anything beautifully written with long treatises on science. She thought plot-driven fiction an abomination, and sf on movies and television beneath her notice.

Although she might have changed that opinion, since her current boyfriend, who had started as Science Fiction's answer to James Joyce, had gotten a job as a story consultant for a major studio. ("A guy has to make a buck," he said to me at the last Worldcon. "Besides, since *Independence Day*, everyone is hot for sf properties.")

She might have changed her opinion, but I doubted it.

I had known Lucinda for a long time. She and I had had a run-in at Con Diego (called Con Digeo by its attendees because of all the typos in the program book) several years back and I had tried, unsuccessfully, to avoid her ever since. Our conversations from that day on had consisted of only two words, uttered in passing.

Asshole, she say.

Bitch, I'd respond.

I sighed, squared my shoulders, and braced myself for the verbal onslaught as I knocked on the door.

Doris answered. She looked grim and shaky. She motioned me inside and closed the door.

The suite smelled of fresh bread, chili, and something foul, something I had never smelled before and wasn't sure I wanted to smell again. We stood in an entry that led to the bathroom on the left, a main room just before me, and a bedroom on the right. The security kid so skinny he was skeletal and a shade of green I'd never seen outside of a blacklight poster, leaned against a faux Louis the Fourteenth table. He had a hand over his mouth and was taking deep breaths, as if to calm his stomach.

"What is it?" I asked.

Doris pointed toward the main room. I lumbered in, cautiously, not sure what to expect. A chocolate pterodactyl hung from the ceiling and flower arrangements that looked vaguely prehistoric stood on every end-table, along with cute little origami triceratops heads. A human-sized tyrannosaurus rex made entirely out of cheese stood on a circular mirror stand in the center of the room. Crock pots filled with chili bubbled on a table leaning against the wall dividing the main room from the bathroom.

"What—?" I started to ask again, and then I saw her.

She was sprawled on the floor, her left hand resting on the glass double doors leading out to the patio. The doors were closed. I cautiously made my way around the cheese dinosaur and the main table, still in the middle of preparations for the night's party, and stopped near her apron-clad torso.

There was no doubt it was Lucinda. She wore a linen pantsuit beneath that apron, and in her right hand she held an apple partially julienned into a stegosaurus. It was her head that was the problem.

It had been stomped flat, crushed into unrecogniz-ability. More gray matter than I would have expected spattered the teal carpet, mixed with more blood than I had ever seen in my life. I swallowed twice, hard, not wanting to repeat the pea soup episode and contaminate the crime scene. Then I cautiously made my way back into the foyer.

"You call the cops?" I asked.

"No!" Doris said. "They'd shut us down."

"Damn straight they'd shut us down," I said. "We have a murderer on the loose here."

The kid moaned and headed toward the bathroom.

I grabbed his arm. "Uh-uh," I said. "Puke in the public restroom. You don't want to contaminate a crime scene."

"Too late," he mumbled, yanked free, and stumbled into the bathroom, kicking the door closed behind him.

"Poor kid," Doris said. "I'm amazed he has any stomach left."

"Listen, Doris, we gotta call the cops." I covered my hand with my sleeve and reached for the black rotary dial on the faux Louis the Fourteenth.

Doris put her hand on mine, forcing the receiver down. "It's Friday afternoon," she said. "Think about what that means."

Eight thousand attendees, all of whom would demand refunds. The hotel, which would sue for breach of contract. The reputation, which would shut down all Los Angeles area conventions for the foreseeable future, not to mention all media cons, not to mention all conventions held in this hotel chain forever.

Millions of dollars, all because Lucinda made someone stomping mad.

"Can't we at least wait until tomorrow?" Doris asked.

Retching sounds echoed from the bathroom. My stomach rolled in sympathy.

"Tomorrow?" I asked. "Don't you remember the party signs that are up all over this convention. For tonight? In this room?"

"Can't we change them to tomorrow night?" she asked. "Then we won't have to refund, and we won't be in breach of contract."

But we would still have the reputation problem, along with another one.

"Tampering with a crime scene is illegal, Doris," I said softly.

"Can't you solve this?" she asked. "Can't you solve this before the cops get here?"

"I've never done a murder investigation before, Doris," I said.

"*Please*," she asked. "If we can give them a suspect, they won't shut us down, and Ruth and I can handle the PR problem, at least long enough to save the con."

"You don't care that a woman has been trampled in her own hotel room?"

Doris crossed her muscular arms. "You really need to ask me that, Spade? I wouldn't be so rude as to ask you."

She could have, though. Because I was upset. Lucinda had her points. She made a mean chocolate soufflé, and she knew more about fannish foods than anyone I had ever met. She also had her moments: the charity auction she ran for literacy at Orycon in the early '90s brought in $5,000 more than usual because she browbeat the attendees into spending more money. And she got them to do it by having them buy signed books.

Sometimes I found myself in complete agreement with Lucinda's arguments.

And that terrified me.

I stared at Doris.

"Will you help us?" she asked.

I sighed. "I won't tamper with the crime scene, and I will meet with the police when they arrive. You will call them from this room and you will make sure that no one else enters here. You'll also keep the kid from talking to anyone but me. If I happen to solve this thing before the police arrive, fine. But I won't go any farther than that. I'm not going to let some murderer run loose because you want to hold a media con honoring one of the lamest movies of all time."

"The special effects were cool." The kid had opened the door to the bathroom. He was now a chalk white.

"But the plot sucked," I said. Then I nodded at Doris. "Call. I'm going to snoop a bit. And don't leave until I tell you to. Got that?"

She nodded and reached for the phone. I stopped her. "Cover your hands with your sleeves. And don't touch anything besides that receiver."

She glared at me, but followed my instructions. I prowled into the bedroom, deciding to talk to the kid after his breath cleared up.

Lucinda, not surprisingly, was a neat freak. She had arrived and unpacked, her clothing hanging on her hangers in the walk-in closet. Each item was separated by tissue paper, and her hats were in boxes on the shelf above. Her shoes were lined up below in neat little rows beneath the matching clothes. She had two wigs on the dressing table, one studded with little plastic dinosaurs—the clear brightly colored kind that bartenders used to put in drinks in the mid-sixties. A silver lamé dress hung from the plant hook in the ceiling. Lucinda had planned to go all out on this party, and it surprised me. She had to be doing a favor for someone. Media cons were beneath her—and while she enjoyed fannish cooking, she hated fannish clothing.

I got back into the foyer as Doris hung up the phone. "I didn't tell them it was a murder," she said.

I mentally shook my head. That would be her problem when the cops arrived. It would be better for all of us if I had some idea what had happened.

"Okay, kid," I said to the security boy, "come into my office and talk to me. And don't touch anything."

The kid's color still hadn't returned. He followed me into Lucinda's bedroom and started to close the door.

"Don't touch," I said. We went deep into the bowels of the room, and stopped near the bed. I knew that Doris would have trouble hearing us from this spot because I had had trouble hearing her on the phone.

"What's your name?" I asked.

"Chad," he said. I raised a single eyebrow, Spocklike. I had never met a kid who worked con security named Chad. Or at least, a kid who worked con security who would admit to being named Chad.

"Okay," I said, "I need to know: what made you come to this room in the first place?"

He wiped his mouth with the back of his hand. That stomach of his was amazingly weak. "I was by the flyer table—that was my post—when these fans came down the stairs and told me they'd heard a huge pounding on the fourth floor. They took me to their room on three and I heard it too, like something really heavy was going to crash through the floor. Then I came up here. The door was open, and I let myself in. It was really quiet. I called out to see if anyone was here, and then I saw the food. I went in to grab a snack and —"

He burped, then covered his mouth, swallowing hard. "Sorry," he said.

"It's all right," I said. "Do you know who these fans were?"

"Not by name," he said. "But they have the room below this one."

And were probably preparing for another party since the room below also had to be a suite. I rubbed my chin in proper detective fashion. I had a conundrum. I need to talk to those fans, but I didn't want to leave Doris alone in the room. Nor did I want anyone else to know what had happened to Lucinda.

Then I realized it didn't matter. Doris had been in the room without me already. I had investigated, and I knew how things looked. I had seen everything but the bathroom, and that could be remedied.

I took the kid back to the foyer. "Wait here," I said, and peered into the bathroom. The kid had already contaminated the crime scene—several times—but there didn't seem to be much to see. The bathtub was still maid-spotless and the counter had Lucinda's make-up and nothing else. The toilet seat was up, one of the towels was askew, and otherwise everything looked fine. It didn't even smell as bad as I thought it would.

"Okay," I said as I emerged. "Let's find those fans. You wait here, Doris, and don't touch anything."

"Don't worry," she said, looking faintly annoyed at the suggestion.

The kid and I slipped into the hallway. The con was filling up. Two women wearing belly dancer skirts and midriff tops, conversed about the proper navel jewel. Five teenage boys compared tattoos. Three grown men, in Klingon boots and armor, adjusted each other's forehead ridges.

The kid and I took the stairs.

The third floor was filled with people in dinosaur costumes. Some were cheap Halloween masks, while others were full-bore papier-mâché or plastic. The costumes looked heavy, they looked hot, and they smelled of glue. I stared at them, mostly at the feet, wondering what kind of pressure a person would need to drive those hard plastic soles through a skull and crush it.

Then we were in front of 3708. The kid knocked on the door. His hand was shaking.

It was opened by a slender woman whose black hair formed perfect Louisa May Alcott ringlets around her face. She wore a lavender satin shirt with purple satin pants, and the outfit somehow looked perfect on her. Her convention badge was clipped to a tiny piece of cardboard inside her shirt's high pocket, so as not to ruin the satin.

"Hi," she said, looking a bit confused.

"Security," the kid said, glancing at me. "Remember? You asked about the big stomping?"

"Oh, yeah." She was staring at me. Her eyes were lavender, like the shirt. I'd never seen eyes like that in person before. Only in photographs of Elizabeth Taylor. "Who're you?"

"I'm from Ops," I said. "Mind if we come in?"

"Why?" She was asking the kid.

"Because when I went upstairs," he said, "I found —"

I kicked him. He shut up.

"He found that he had a few more questions to ask you," I said. "Mind if we come in."

"No," she said. "I guess not."

She got out of our way, and we stepped into the foyer. It exactly matched the suite above, only here the carpet was brown. Two men sat in the suite's living room. They looked vaguely familiar. They stood as they saw us come in.

"Something wrong?" the first one asked.

He was tall and muscular—those fakey kind of muscles that come from too much health club, and too much low-fat food. His shirt was unbuttoned below the navel, revealing a washboard stomach, and his bare feet looked manicured. His companion wore ripped jeans and a *Star Trek* t-shirt, but unless I missed my guess, his hair had been permed.

Interesting look, for fans. It looked a little too Hollywood, a little too put together, for my tastes. Maybe these folks were slumming.

"You guys with the convention?" I asked.

"What's this all about?" T-Shirt asked. He had his hands on his hips. Same fakey muscles, and he didn't look as if he had ever cracked a book. But, I reminded myself, this was a media con. Folks here didn't have to crack books, even though most of them did.

"Of course we're with the convention," the woman said, and tugged gently on her badge as if to prove it.

"What's your interest?" I asked. "Filking?"

"Excuse me," Manicured asked. His face flamed and he looked insulted.

"Fill-king," the kid said, "not fucking."

Interesting comment, I thought, but I didn't look at him. "Pipe down, Chad," I said. "What are you guys doing at the con?"

"Anyone can come," the woman said, apparently realizing that my questions had more importance than the guys were giving them credit for. "Right?"

"Of course," I said, "but usually people have special reasons for attending. What are yours?"

"We like dinosaurs," T-Shirt said.

"Fascinating," I said in my best Spock voice. No one laughed, even though most fans usually did. My best Spock voice was pretty damn good. "So what's your favorite dinosaur? A plugosaurus or a brontodacdyl?"

"All of 'em," T-Shirt said.

"Hmmm," I said. "Hear you had some noise problems."

"Yeah, man, sounded like weird pounding upstairs," Manicured said. "Like someone was trying to punch a hole in the floor."

"Sounds serious," I said. "Will someone move that chair over here?" I pointed to a square wooden chair that seemed to be the sturdiest thing in the room. T-Shirt moved the chair to the place I pointed to, right next to the balcony doors.

"Spot me, Chad, will you?" I asked as I climbed up.

"Ah, um, ah, you might want me to do that," he said.

"No need," I said, even though the chair was groaning under my weight. I reached up and removed the ceiling panel. Gobs of dust and dirt rained on me, and I had to clear a spider web, but after that I had a pretty good glimpse of the space between the ceiling and the floor above.

"Looks normal," I said, and to my surprise, it did. I put the tile back. "You guys are safe."

"That's it?" the woman asked. "That's all? It sounded wretched up there."

"It was," Chad said. I braced myself on his shoulder and squeezed as I got down. It shut him up again.

"That's it," I said cheerfully. "I hope you have a good con."

"Ah, thanks," T-Shirt said. He was frowning at me.

The kid and I left. The dino costumes flooded the hall. The newer ones looked even more realistic than the earlier ones. Especially the Spielbergian velociraptors. All terrifyingly icky except for the guy wearing blue jeans and a tie-dye brontosaurus head. And the inevitable tot dressed as Barney.

One glance at the elevator told me we weren't going back to the fourth floor that way. Too crowded. It also meant the cops wouldn't come up very quickly when they arrived.

"Where to now?" the kid asked.

I didn't answer. I was feeling pretty annoyed with him. Pretty annoyed with the whole thing, really. I wanted to get back to my Ops computer with its lovely numbers and forget I had ever gotten involved with this detecting business.

Even if I was good at it.

We took the stairs and I was puffing by the time we reached the fourth floor. I hadn't had this much exercise in weeks. And I was moving faster than I liked.

Most of the dino costumes were on the third floor. Regular con-goers littered the fourth. None of them looked like the three ringers downstairs.

I shave-and-a-haircut knocked on 4708. Doris answered immediately. "What took you so long?"

I didn't answer. As I came in, I asked, "Did Lucinda know I was coming to Dinocon?"

"How should I know?" Doris asked.

I glared at her.

She sighed, exasperated. "Probably. If she was looking. You would have been hard to miss since your name was in the con-com listing in all the progress reports. Why?"

I had my suspicions. I made my way back into the suite's main room.

"Hey!" the kid said. "What're you doing?"

His voice had gotten increasingly shrill. I ignored him. I made my way to the body, and, just as I remembered, the floor didn't sag under my considerable weight.

I knelt beside the body. The gray matter and blood were drying in a perfect arch.

"Hey!" the kid yelled. "You said no tampering."

"Grab him, Doris," I said through my teeth. He was getting on my nerves. This whole thing was.

I grabbed the right wrist, dislodging the julienned stegosaurus, and felt—plastic. Soft, lifelike, fake plastic.

"Bitch," I mumbled. I half expected the crushed dummy to mumble "asshole" in return. Then, louder, I said, "Doris, did you call 911?"

She didn't answer. I turned. She was frowning at me. "Doris?"

She flushed. "No," she said. "I called the regular line. I wanted to give you as much time as possible."

Her caution had worked to our advantage. "Call and cancel," I said. "Then break that kid's arm if he doesn't tell you where Lucinda is."

"Lucinda—!"

"Just do it." First time I'd ever understood the sense of a Nike ad.

She twisted the kid's arm up behind his back. Within seconds, he was screaming, "Executive Suite! Executive Suite!"

I got up and walked over to him. "Key," I said.

He handed me a specially marked executive floor key. "Come on, Doris," I said. "Keep a good grip on this kid and commandeer us an elevator."

She did exactly as she was told.

***

ON THE WAY UP, I explained the whole thing, and the kid wisely said nothing, confirming all my suspicions. I was trying to contain my anger, because this thing had just become personal.

And to think I would have mourned the bitch if that had truly been her on the floor below.

You see, the plan was simple: the execution was hard. Lucky for Lucinda that her boyfriend had his new job in Hollywood and even luckier for her that most special effects guys are also sf nerds. Ironic that she needed media people to tamper with a media con. But Lucinda had always been a bit dim when it came to irony.

And, apparently, detail, at least non-food related detail.

First there was the fannish clothing. No matter what kind of theme party Lucinda gave, she never, ever dressed in fannish clothes. No wigs decorated with little plastic dinosaurs, no silver lamé dress. She might have consented to work a media con, but she would never have given up her stylishly proper clothing. She planned the perfect media party, all right, down to the clothes, forgetting that she would never, ever wear those clothes because, of course, she didn't plan to.

But that wasn't the only detail that bothered me. The three "fans" on the floor below had been extras in a straight-to-video sf release that I'd been watching at home a few nights before the con. I would have made them as non-skiffy folk anyway. All science fiction fans—media and lit alike—know the difference between a real dinosaur and a made-up one.

And then there was Chad, clearly another actor for hire. Except he overdid the vomit bit, and the bathroom smelled as if the maid had just left. Lucinda probably hadn't counted on the strength of my sniffer.

But she had counted on me. In fact, I had been the center of her plan. Without me, it wouldn't have worked. She knew that I knew better than to tamper with a crime scene, no matter how great the temptation. She knew that I had a healthy respect for the authorities and that I would insist on cops being present.

And she knew that the cops would see this for the hoax it was. She would appear at the right moment, blame the convention for overreacting to her little party, piss off the cops just enough to get the whole con shut down. The hotel chain would have been angry, the attendees would have demanded refunds, and the whole cascade effect that Doris had foreseen when she first saw that body would have occurred. Media cons, not just in LA, but all over the country would have suffered, and possibly died.

Lucinda's little stunt would have caused more damage than the murder. It was sabotage, served cold.

***

WHEN WE REACHED the executive suite, Doris made the kid open the door. Lucinda saw him, stood up, and cooed. She was dressed for her act in a white sheath that accented her lightly tanned skin and golden hair.

When she saw us, her eyes widened.

"You bitch," Doris said, blowing my line and letting go of the kid. He started to back away, but I shoved him forward and closed the door behind us.

"Back off, Doris," I said. "She's mine. There won't be any cops, Lucinda. You won't ruin this convention."

"I'm going to see that you're banned from cons forever. I'm going to make sure that your name is taken out of the Fannish Directory. I'm going to—"

"For what? For a little party I planned to throw for some friends?" Lucinda asked. "Don't you think it rather cute? I do."

"You—"

Doris lunged for her, and I caught her, staggering a bit under her power. The kid bee-lined for the bathroom, fear making his intentions real this time.

"Go to Ops," I said to Doris. "Tell them everything is fine. I can take it from here."

"I'm going to get you," Doris said, but she listened to me. She knew as well as I did that strange things happened at sf conventions, and that there was no proving malicious intent here.

Knowing about it was something else.

"Misunderstandings are so tragic, Doris," Lucinda said, blinking her blue eyes guilelessly.

Doris growled and disappeared out the door. I stood in front of Lucinda. "Media cons aren't your style."

She smiled. It was sweet as rhubarb pie. "They're not yours either."

"I don't see anything wrong with people having fun. I'm a bit more open-minded than you, Lucinda. I believe people can enjoy reading and watching movies. I believe there's room in fandom for both."

"You're so naive," she said. "These cons are so anti-literature. They appeal only to the ignorant. People who don't understand real science, or real science fiction."

"I think people who think they guard pure science fiction may not understand real science or real science fiction either," I said pointedly.

"Good god," she said, "a philosophical discussion when I have a party to finish."

"It seems strange to me that you'd put on a party here, Lucinda."

She shrugged. "I thought I'd give these people the opportunity to come to a lit-con and see what they were missing."

"So kind of you," I said.

She smoothed her dress. "We all do what we can in the circumstances provided."

At that moment, I almost told her what tripped her up. I almost told her that it was her lack of scientific knowledge, her lack of understanding of forensic science that had destroyed her. First, the splatter had been too pretty, too uniform. Second, and more importantly, the type of force it took to stomp out someone's brains would have caused damage to the plywood floor. Damage someone of my weight would have felt in loose boards or groaning wood.

But I didn't. Why give her the ammunition? She might try again someday.

"Am I excused?" she asked brightly.

"There is no excuse for you, Lucinda," I said in my best fannish manner, and moved out of her way.

***

THE BANE OF THE non-licensed investigator is that we have no real authority. We can't arrest. Worse yet, people with authority often look down their noses at us.

So we are forced to take some matters into our own hands.

Lucinda, misguided as she was, was clever. Who could prove that the panic the kid, Doris, and I felt was anything more than a product of our own imaginations? She would say that she had planned a perfect party, and we had nearly ruined it.

In fact, that night, she did carry off the party with full aplomb. She did change the victim from her clone to that of a lawyer, in keeping with *Jurassic Park* (the movie) tradition, and she did pour ice in the bathtub, but those were the only changes she made. The party was the hit of the convention, and became the talk of sf—both media- and literature-oriented—for years to come. It was, in its own way, the Woodstock of science fiction. Eventually everyone who was anyone claimed they had been there, even if they had been clear across the country at the time.

Everyone who was anyone except me.

You see, I was in Ops, checking the computer records. We had an unexplained power failure just as I was transferring Lucinda's credit card information from her con file into an active file so that we could bill her account. Unfortunately, the accident caused blips in her credit record that cascaded down the system and destroyed her credit rating for the next year. She had to defend and deny and repair, all of which took time away from cons and con parties, and fandom.

And somehow she got it in her pretty little head that this would happen again if she ever attempted to sabotage—even accidentally—a major convention again.

Misunderstandings are so tragic.

But we all do what we can in the circumstances provided.

Monuments to the Dead

THE CALIFORNIA PERSPECTIVE:
REFLECTIONS ON MT. RUSHMORE
by
L. Emilia Sunlake

*The union of these four presidents carved on the face
of the everlasting hills of South Dakota will contribute a distinctly national monument. It will be decid-
edly American in its conception, in its magnitude, in
its meaning, and altogether worthy of our country.*
—Calvin Coolidge at the dedication
of Mt. Rushmore in 1927

CARS CRAWL ALONG HIGHWAY 16. The hot summer sun
reflects off shiny bumper stickers, most plastered with
the mementos of tourist travel: Sitting Bull Crystal Cave,
Wall Drug, and I (heart) anything from terriers to West
Virginia. The windows are open, and children lean out,
trying to see magic shimmering in the heat visions on

the pavement. The locals say the traffic has never been like this, that even in the height of tourist season, the cars can at least go thirty miles an hour. Kenny, the photographer, and I have been sitting in this sticky heat for most of the afternoon, moving forward a foot at a time, sharing a Diet Coke, and hoping the story will be worth the aggravation.

I have never been to the Black Hills before. Until I started writing regularly for the slick magazines, I had never been out of California, and even then my outside assignments were rare. Usually I wrote about things close to home: the history of Simi Valley, for instance, or the relationships between the Watts riot and the Rodney King riot twenty-five years later. When *American Observer* sent me to South Dakota, they asked me to write from a California perspective. What they will get is a white, middle-class, female California perspective. Despite my articles on the cultural diversity of my home state, *American Observer*—published in New York—continues to think that all Californians share the same opinions, beliefs, and outlooks.

Of course, now, sitting in bumper-to-bumper traffic in the dense heat, I feel right at home.

Kenny has brought a lunch—tuna fish—which, in the oppressive air has a rancid two-days dead odor. He eats with apparent gusto, while I sip on soda and try to peer ahead. Kenny says nothing. He is a slender man with long black hair and wide dark eyes. I chose him because he is the best photographer I have ever met, a man who can capture the heart of a moment in a single image. He also rarely speaks, a trait I usually enjoy, but one I have found annoying on this long afternoon as we wait in the trail of cars.

He sees me lean out the window for the fifth time in the last minute. "Why don't you interview some of the tourists?"

I shake my head and he goes back to his sandwich. The tourists aren't the story. The story waits for us at the end of this road, at the end of time.

***

When I think of Mount Rushmore, I think of Cary Grant clutching the lip of a stone-faced Abraham Lincoln with Eva Saint-Marie beside him, looking over her shoulder at the drop below. The movie memory has the soft fake tones of early color or perhaps early colorization—the pale blues that don't exist in the natural world, the red lipstick that is five shades too red. As a child, I wanted to go to the monument and hang off a president myself. As an adult, I disdained tourist traps, and had avoided all of them with amazing ease.

Later, I tell my husband of this, and he corrects me: Cary Grant was hanging off George Washington's forehead. Kenny disagrees: he believes Grant crawled around Teddy Roosevelt's eyes. A viewing of *North by Northwest* would settle this disagreement, but I saw the movie later, as an adult, and found the special effects not so special, and the events contrived. If Cary Grant hadn't stupidly pulled the knife from a dead man's body, there would have been no movie. The dead man, the knife, were an obvious set-up, and Grant's character fell right into the trap.

Appropriate, I think, for a Californian to have a cinematic memory of Mount Rushmore. As I study the history, however, I find it much more compelling, and frighteningly complex.

***

THE BLACK HILLS are as old as any geological formation in North America. They rise out of the flat lands on the Wyoming and Dakota borders, mysterious shadowy hills that are cut out of the dust. The dark pine trees made the hills look black from a distance. The Paha Sapa, or the Black Hills, were the center of the world for the surrounding tribes. They used the streams and lakes hidden by the trees; they hunted game in the wooded areas; and in the summer, the young men went to the sacred points on a four-day vision quest that would shape and focus the rest of their lives.

According to Lakota tribal legend, the hills were a reclining female figure from whose breasts flowed life. The Lakota went to the hills as a child went to its mother's arms. In 1868, the United States government signed a treaty with the Indians, granting them "absolute and undisturbed use of the Great Sioux Reservation," which included the Black Hills. Terms of the treaty included the line, "No white person or persons shall be permitted to settle upon or occupy any portion of the territory, or without the consent of the Indians to pass through the same."

White persons have been trespassing ever since.

***

FINALLY I CAN STAND the smell of tuna no longer. I push the door open on the rental car and stand. My jeans and t-shirt cling to my body—I am not used to humid heat. I walk along the edge of the highway, peering into cars, seeing pale face after pale face. Most of the tourists ignore me, but a few watch hesitantly, as they fear that I am going to pull a gun and leap into their car beside them.

Everyone knows of the troubles in the Black Hills, and most people have brought their families despite the dangers. Miracles only happen once in a lifetime.

I see no one I want to speak to until I pass a red pickup truck. Its paint is chipped, and the frame is pocked with rust. A Native American woman sits inside, a black braid running down her back. She is dressed as I am, except that sweat does not stain her white t-shirt, and she wears heavy turquoise rings on all of her fingers.

"Excuse me," I say. "Are you heading to Mount Rushmore?"

She looks at me, her eyes hooded and dark. Two little boys sleep in the cab, their bodies propped against each other like puppies. A full jug of bottled water sits at her feet, and on the boys' side of the cab, empty pop cans line up like soldiers. "Yes," she says. Her voice is soft.

I introduce myself and explain my assignment. She does not respond, staring at me as if I am speaking in a foreign tongue. "May I talk with you for a little while?"

"No." Again, she speaks softly, but with a finality that brooks no disagreement.

I thank her for her time, shove my hands in my pockets and walk back to the car. Kenny is standing outside of it, the passenger door open. His camera is draped around his neck, reflecting sunlight, and he holds a plastic garbage bag in his hand. He is picking up litter from the roadside—smashed Pepsi cups and dirt-covered MacDonald's bags.

"Lack of respect," he says, when he sees me watching him, "shows itself in little ways."

***

LACK OF RESPECT shows itself in larger ways too: In great stone faces carved on a mother's breast; in broken treaties; in broken bodies bleeding on the snow. The indignities continue into our lifetimes—children ripped from their parents and put into schools that force them to renounce old ways; mysterious killings and harassment arrests; and enforced poverty unheard of even in our inner cities. The stories are frightening and hard to comprehend, partly because they are true. I grasp them only through books—from Dee Brown to Peter Matthiessen, from Charles A. Eastman (Ohiyesa) to Vine Deloria Jr.—and through film—from documentary to documentary (usually produced by P.C. white men), ending with *Incident at Ogala*, and from fictional accounts (starring non-natives, of course) from *Little Big Man* to *Thunderheart*.

Some so-called wise person once wrote that women have the capacity to understand all of American society: we have lived in a society dominated by white men, and so had to understand their perspective to survive; we were abused and treated as property within our own homes, having no rights and no recourse under the law, so we understand blacks, Hispanics, and Native Americans. But I stand on this road, outside a luxury car that I rented with my gold Mastercard, and I do not understand what it is like to be a defeated people, living among the victors, watching them despoil all that I value and all that I believe in.

Instead of empathy, I have white liberal guilt. When I stared across the road into the darkness of that truck cab, I felt the Native American woman's eyes assessing me. My sons sleep in beds with Ninja Turtles decorating the sheets; they wear Nikes and tear holes in their shirts on purpose. They fight over the Nintendo and the remote controls. I buy dolphin-safe tuna, and pay attention to food boycotts, but I shop in a grocery store filled with light and choices. And while I understand that the fruits of my life were purchased with the lives of people I have never met, I tell myself there is nothing I can do to change that. What is past is past.

But the past determines who we are, and it has led to this startling future.

***

I REMEMBER THE MOMENT with the clarity my parents have about the Kennedy assassination, the clarity my generation associates with the destruction of the space shuttle Challenger. I was waiting in my husband's Ford Bronco outside the recreation center. The early June day was hot in a California desert sort of way—the dry heat of an oven, heat that prickles but does not invade the skin. My youngest son pulled open the door and crawled in beside me, bringing with him dampness and filling the air with the scents of chlorine and institutional soap. He tossed his wet suit and towel on the floor, fastened his seatbelt and said, "Didja hear? Mount Rushmore disappeared."

I smiled at him, thinking it amazing the way ten-year-old little boy minds worked—I hadn't even realized he knew what Mount Rushmore was—and he frowned at my response.

"No, really," he said, voice squeaking with sincerity. "It did. Turn on the news."

Without waiting for me, he flicked on the radio and scanned to the all news channel.

"…not an optical illusion," a female voice was saying. "The site now resembles those early photos, taken around the turn of the century, before the work on the monument began."

Through the hour-long drive home, we heard the story again and again. No evidence of a bomb, no sign of the remains of the great stone faces. No rubble, nothing. Hollywood experts spoke about the possibilities of an illusion this grand, but all agreed that the faces would be there, behind the illusion, at least available to the sense of touch.

My hands were shaking by the time we pulled into the driveway of our modified ranch home. My son, whose assessment had gone from "pretty neat" to "kinda scary" within the space of the drive (probably from my grim and silent reaction), got out of the car without taking his suit and disappeared into the backyard to consult with his older brother. I took the suit, and went inside, cleaning up by rote as I made my way to the bedroom we used as a library.

The quote I wanted, the quote that had been running through my mind during the entire drive, was there on page 93 of the 1972 Simon and Schuster edition of Richard Erdos' *Lame Deer: Seeker of Visions*:

> *One man's shrine is another man's cemetery, except that now a few white folks are also getting tired of having to look at this big paperweight curio [Mount Rushmore]. We can't get away from it. You could make a lovely mountain into a great paperweight, but can you make it into a wild, natural mountain again? I don't think you have the know-how for that.*
> —John Fire Lame Deer

Lame Deer went on to say that white men, who had the ability to fly to the moon, should have the know-how to take the faces off the mountain.

But no one had the ability to take the faces off overnight.

No one.

***

WE FINALLY REACH THE SITE around 5 p.m. Kenny has snapped three rolls of film on our approach. He began shooting about 60 miles away, the place where, they tell me, the faces were first visible. I try to envision the shots as he sees them: the open mouths, the shocked expressions. I know Kenny will capture the moment, but I also know he will be unable to capture the thing which holds me.

The sound.

The rumble of low conversation over the soft roar of car engines. The shocked tones, rising and falling like a wave on the open sea.

I see nothing ahead of me except the broad expanse of a mountain outlined in the distance. I have not seen the faces up close and personal. I cannot tell the difference. But the others can. Pheromones fill the air, and I can almost taste the excitement. It grows as we pull into the over-crowded parking lot, as we walk to the visitors center that still shows its 1940s roots.

Kenny disappears into the crowd. I walk to the first view station, and stare at a mountain, at a granite surface smooth as water-washed stone. A chill runs along my back. At the base, uniformed people with cameras and surveying equipment check the site. Other uniformed people move along the top of the mount; it appears that they have just pulled someone up on the equivalent of a window-washers pull cart.

All the faces here are white, black or Asian—non-Native. We pass the Native woman as we drove into the parking lot. Two men, wearing army fatigues and carrying rifles had stopped the truck. She was leaning out of the cab, speaking wearily to them, and Kenny made me slow as we passed. He eavesdropped in his intense way, and then nodded once.

"She will be all right," he said, and nothing more.

The hair on my arms has prickled. T.V. crews film from the edge of the parking lot. A middle aged man, his stomach parting the buttons on his short-sleeved white shirt, aims a video camera at the site. I am not a nature lover. Within minutes, I am bored with the changed mountain. Miracle, yes, but now that my eyes have confirmed it, I want to get on with the story.

Inside the visitor's center is an ancient diorama on the building of Mt. Rushmore. The huge sculpted busts of George Washington, Abraham Lincoln, Thomas Jefferson, and Theodore Roosevelt took 14 years to complete. Gutzon Borglum (Bore-glum, how appropriate) designed the monument, which was established in 1925, during our great heedless prosperity, and finished in 1941, after the Crash, the Depression and at the crest of America's involvement in World War II. The diorama makes only passing mention—in a cheerful "aren't they cute?" 1950s way—to the importance of the Mount to the Native tribes. There is no acknowledgment of the fact that when the monument was being designed, the Lakota had filed a court claim asking for financial compensation for the theft of the Black Hills. A year after the completion of the monument, the courts denied the claim. No acknowledgment of the split between native peoples that occurred when the case was revived in the 1950s—the split over financial compensation and return of the land itself.

Nor is there any mention of the bloody history of the surrounding area that continued into the 1970s with the American Indian Movement, the death of two FBI agents and an Indian on the Pine Ridge Reservation, the resulting trials, the violence that marked the decade, and the attempted take-over of the Black Hills themselves.

In the true tradition of a conquering force, of an occupying army, all mention of the on-going war has been obliterated.

But not forgotten. The army, with their rifles, are out in force. Several young boys, their lean muscled frames outlined in their black t-shirts and fatigue pants, sit at the blond wood tables. Others sit outside, rifles leaning against their chairs. We were not stopped as we entered the parking lot—Kenny claims our trunk is too small to hold a human being—but several others were.

One of the soldiers is getting himself a drink from the overworked waitress behind the counter. I stop beside him. He is only a few years older than my oldest son, and the ferocity of the soldier's clothes make him look even younger. His skin is still pockmarked with acne, his teeth crooked and yellowed from lack of care. Things have not changed from my youth. It is still the children of the poor who receive the orders to die for patriotism, valor, and the American Way.

"A lot of tension here," I say.

He takes his ice tea from the waitress and pours half a cup of sugar into it. "It'd be easier if there weren't no tourists." Then he flushes. "Sorry, lady."

I reassure him that he hasn't offended me, and I explain my purpose.

"We ain't supposed to talk to the press." He shrugs.

"I won't use your name," I say. "And it's for a magazine that won't be published for a month, maybe two months from now."

"Two months anything can happen."

True enough, which is why I have been asked to capture this moment with the vision of an outsider. I know my editor has already asked a white Dakota correspondent to write as well, and she has received confirmation that at least one Native American author will contribute an essay. In this age of cynicism, a miracle is the most important event of our time.

The boy sits at an empty table and pulls out a chair for me. His arms are thick, tanned, and covered with fine white hairs. His fingers are long, slender and ringless, his nails clean. He doesn't look at me as he speaks.

"They sent us up here right when the whole thing started," he said, "and we was told not to let no Indians up here. Some of our guys, they been combing the woods for Indians, making sure that this ain't some kind of front for some special action. I don't like it. The guys are trigger happy, and with all these tourists, I'm afraid that someone's going to do something, and get shot. We ain't going to mean for it to happen. It'll be an accident, but it'll happen just the same."

He drinks his tea in several noisy slurps, tells me a bit about his family—his father, one of the few casualties of the Gulf War, his mother remarried to a foreman of a dying assembly plant in Michigan, his sister, newly married to a career army officer, and himself, his dreams for a real life without a hand-to-mouth income when he leaves the army. He never expected to search cars at the entrance to a National Park, and the miracle makes him nervous.

"I think it's some kind of Indian trick," he says. "You know, a decoy to get us all pumped up and focused here while they attack somewhere else."

This boy, who grew up poor hundreds of miles away, and who probably never gave Native Americans a second thought, is now speaking the language of conquerors, conquerors at the end of an empire, who feel the power slipping through their fingers.

He leaves to return to his post. I speak with a few tourists, but learn nothing interesting. It is as if the Virgin Mary has appeared at Lourdes—everyone wants to be one of the first to experience the miracle.

I am half-surprised no one has set up a faith healing station—a bit of granite from the holy mountain, and all ailments will be cured.

The light is turning silver with approaching twilight. My stomach is rumbling, but I do not want one of the hot dogs that has been twirling in the little case all afternoon. The oversized salted pretzels are gone, and the grill is caked with grease. The waitress herself looks faded, her dishwater blond hair slipping from its bun, her uniform covered with sweat stains and ketchup. I go to find Kenny, but cannot see him in the crowds. Finally I see him, on a path just past the parking lot, sitting beneath a scraggly pine tree, talking with an elderly man.

The elderly man's hair is white and short, but his face has a photogenic cragginess that most WASP photographers find appealing in Native Americans. As I approach, he touches Kenny's arm, then slips down the path and disappears into the growing darkness.

"Who was that?" I ask as I stop in front of Kenny. I am standing over him, looming, and the question feels like an interrogation, as if I am asking for information I do not deserve. Kenny grabs his camera and takes a picture of me. When we view it later, we will see different things: he will see the formation of light and shadow into a tired irritable woman, made more irritable by an occurrence she cannot explain or understand, and I will see the teachers from my childhood enforcing some arbitrary rule on the playground.

When he is finished, he holds out his hand and I pull him to his feet. We walk back to the car in silence, and he never answers my question.

***

SPECULATION IS RIFE IN RAPID CITY. The woman at the Super Eight on the Interstate hands out her opinion with the old-fashioned room keys. "They're using some new-fangled technology and trying to scare us," she says, her voice roughened by her six-pack a day habit. Wisps of smoke curl around the Mt. Rushmore mugs and the tour-ist brochures that fill the dark wood lobby. "They know if that monument goes away there's really no reason for folks to stop here."

She never explains who she means by "they." In this room filled with white people, surrounded by memen-toes of the "Old West," the meaning of "they" is imme-diately clear.

As it is downtown. The stately old Victorian homes and modified farm houses attest to this city's roots. Some older buildings still stand in the center of town, dwarfed by newer hotels built to swallow the tourist trade. Usually, the locals tell me, the clientele is mixed here. Some busi-ness people show for various conventions and must frat-ernize with the bikers who have a convention of their own in nearby Sturgis every summer. The tourists are the most visible: with their video cameras and tow-headed children, they visit every sight available from the Geology Museum to the Sioux Indian Museum. We all check our maps and make no comment over roads named after Indian fighters like Philip Sheridan.

In a dusky bar whose owner does not want named in this "or any" article, a group of elderly men share a drink before they toddle off to their respective homes. They too have theories, and they're willing to talk with a young female reporter from California.

"You don't remember the seventies," says Terry, a loud-voiced, balding man who lives in a nearby retirement home. "Lots of young reporters like you, honey, and them AIM people, stirring up trouble. There was more guards at Rushmore than before or since. We always thought they'd blow up that monument. They hate it, you know. Say we've defaced—" (and they all laugh at the pun) "—defaced their sacred hills."

"I say they lost the wars fair and square," says Rudy. He and his wife of 45 years live in a six-bedroom Victorian house on the corner of one of the tree-lined streets. "No sense whining about it. Time they start learning to live like the rest of us."

"Always thought they would bomb that monument." Max, a former lieutenant in the Army, fought "the Japs" at Guadalcanal, a year that marked the highlight of his life. "And now they have."

"There was no bomb," says Jack, a former college professor who still wears tweed blazers with patches on the elbows. "Did you hear any explosion? Did you?"

The others don't answer. It becomes clear they have had this conversation every day since the faces disappeared. We speak a bit more, then I leave in search of other opinions. As I reach the door, Jack catches my arm.

"Young lady," he says, ushering me out into the darkness of the quiet street. "We've been living the Indian wars all our lives. It's hard to ignore when you live beside a prison camp. I'm not apologizing for my friends—but it's hard to live here, to see all that poverty, to know that we—our government—causes that devastation because the Indians—the natives—want to live their own way. It's a strange prison we've built for them. They can escape if they want to renounce everything they are."

In his voice I hear the thrum of the professor giving a lecture. "What did you teach?" I ask.

He smiles, and in the reflected glare of the bar's neon sign, I see the unlined face of the man he once was. "History," he says. "And I tell you, living here, I have learned that history is not a deep dusty thing of the past, but part of the air we breathe each and every day."

His words send a shiver through me. I thank him for his time and return to my rented car. As I drive to my hotel, I pass the Rushmore Mall—a flat late 70s creation that has sprawled to encompass other stores. The mall is closing, and hundreds of cars pull away, oblivious to the strangeness that has happened only a few miles outside the city.

***

By morning, the police, working in cooperation with the FBI, have captured a suspect. But they will not let any of the reporters talk with him, nor will they release his name, his race or anything else about him. They don't even specify the charges.

"How can they?" asks the reporter for *The New York Times* over an overpriced breakfast of farm-fresh eggs, thick bacon and wheat toast at a local diner. "They don't know what happened to the monument. So they charge him with making the faces disappear? Unauthorized use of magic in an un-American fashion?"

"Who says it's magic?" the CNN correspondent asks.

"You explain it," says the man from the *Wall Street Journal*. "I touched the rock face yesterday. Nothing is carved there. It feels like nothing ever was."

The reporters are spooked, and the explanations they share among themselves have the ring of mysticism. That mysticism does not reach the American people, however. On the air, in the pages of the country's respected newspapers and magazines, the talk revolves around possible technical explanations for the disappearance of the faces. Any whisper of the unexplainable and the show, the interviewee, and the story are whisked off the air.

It is as if we are afraid of things beyond our ken.

In the afternoon, I complain to Kenny that, aside from the woman in the truck and the man he talked to near the monument, I have seen no natives. The local and national native organizations have been strangely silent. National spokespeople for the organizations have arrived in Rapid City—only to disappear behind some kind of protective walls. Even people who revel in the limelight have avoided it on this occasion.

"They have no explanations either," Kenny says with such surety that I glare at him. He has been talking with the natives while I have not.

Finally he shrugs. "They have found a place in the Black Hills that is *theirs*. They believe something wonderful is about to happen."

"Take me there," I say.

He shakes his head. "I cannot. But I can bring someone to you."

***

KENNY DRIVES THE RENTAL CAR off the Interstate, down back roads so small as to not be on the map. Old faded signs for now-defunct cafes and secret routes to the Black Hills Caverns give the area a sense of Twilight Zone mystery. Out here, the towns have names that send chills down my back, names like Mystic and Custer. Kenny leaves me at a roadside cafe that looks as if it closed when Kennedy was president. The windows are boarded up, but the door swings open to reveal a dusty room filled with rat prints and broken furniture. Someone has removed the grill and the rest of the equipment, leaving gaping holes in the sideboards, but the counter remains, a testament to what might have been a once-thriving business.

There are tables near the gravel parking lot outside. They have been wiped clean, and one bears cup rings that look to be fairly recent. The cafe may be closed, but the tables are still in use. I wipe off a bench and sit down, a little unnerved that Kenny has left me in this desolate place alone—with only a cellular phone for comfort.

The sun is hot as it rises in the sky, and I am thankful for the bit of shade provided by the building's overhang. No cars pass on this road, and I am beginning to feel as if I have reached the edge of nowhere.

I have brought my laptop, and I spend an hour making notes from the day's conversations: trying to place them in a coherent order so that this essay will make sense. It has become clearer and clearer to me that—unless I have the luck of a fictional detective—I will find no answers before my Monday deadline. I will submit only a series of impressions and guesses based on my own observations of a fleeting moment. I suppose that is why the *American Observer* hired me instead of an investigative reporter, so that I can capture this moment of mystery in my white California way.

Finally I hear the moan of a car engine, and relief loosens the tension in my shoulders. I have not, until this moment, realized how tense the quiet has made me. Sunlight glares off the car's new paint job, and the springs squeak as the wheels catch the potholes that fill the road. Kenny's face is obscured by the windshield, but as the car turns in the parking lot, I recognize his passenger as the elderly man I had seen the day before.

The car stops and I stand. Kenny gets out and leads the elderly man to me. I introduce myself and thank the man for joining us. He nods in recognition but does not give me his name. "I am here as a favor to Little Hawk," he says, nodding at Kenny. "Otherwise I would not speak to you."

Kenny is fiddling with his camera. He looks no different, and yet my vision of him has suddenly changed. We never discussed his past or mine for that matter. In California, a person either proclaims his heritage loudly or receives his privacy. I am definitely not an investigator. I did not know that my cameraman has ties in part of the Dakotas.

I close my laptop as I sit. The old man sits beside me. Silver mixes with the black hair in his braid. I have seen his face before. Later I will look it up and discover what it looked like when it was young, when he was making the news in the 1970s for his association with AIM.

I open my mouth to ask a question and he raises his hand, shaking his head slightly. Behind us, a bird chirps. A drop of sweat runs down my back.

"I know what you will ask," he says. "You want me to give you the answers. You want to know what is happening, and how we caused it."

My questions are not as blunt as that, but he has the point. I have fallen into the same trap as the locals. I am blaming the natives because I see no other explanation.

"When he gave his farewell address to the Lakota," the old man said in a ringing voice accustomed to stories, "he said, 'As a child I was taught the Supernatural Powers were powerful and could do strange things....

This was taught me by the wise men and the shamans. They taught me that I could gain their favor by being kind to my people and brave before my enemies; by telling the truth and living straight; by fighting for my people and their hunting grounds…'

"All my life we have fought, Ms. Sunlake, and we have tried to live the old path. But I was taught as a child that we had been wicked, that we were living in sin, and that we must accept Christ as our Savior, for in Him is the way.

"In Him, my people found death over a hundred years ago, at Wounded Knee. In Him, we have watched our Mother ravaged and our hunting grounds ruined. And I wish I could say that by renouncing Him and His followers we have begun this change. But I cannot."

The bird has stopped chirping. His voice echoes in the silence. Kenny's camera whirs, once, twice, and I think of the old superstition that Crazy Horse and some of the others held, that a camera stole the soul. This old man does not have that fear.

He puts out a hand and touches my arm. His knuckles are large and swollen with age. A twisted white scar runs from his wrist to his elbow. "We have heard that there are many buffalo on the Great Plain, and that the water is receding from Lake Powell. We are together now in the Hills, waiting and following the old traditions. Little Hawk has been asked to join us, but he will not."

I glance at Kenny. He is holding his camera chest high and staring at the old man, tears in his eyes. I look away.

"In our search for answers, we have forgotten that Red Cloud is right," the old man said. "*Taku Wakan* are powerful and can do strange things."

He stands and I stand with him. "But why now?" I ask. "Why not a hundred years ago? Two hundred years ago?"

The look he gives me is sad. I am still asking questions, unwilling to accept.

"Perhaps," he said, "the *Taku Wakan* know that if they wait much longer the People will be gone, and the Earth will belong to madmen." Then he nods at Kenny and they walk to the car.

"I will be back soon," Kenny says. I sit back down and try to write this meeting down in my laptop. What I cannot convey is the sense of unease with which it left me, the feeling that I have missed more than I could ever see.

***

"WHY DON'T YOU GO WITH THEM?" I ask Kenny as we drive back to Rapid City.

For a long time, he does not answer me. He stares straight ahead at the narrow road, the fading white lines illuminated only by his headlights. He had come for me just before dark. The mosquitoes had risen in the twilight, and I had felt that the essay and I would die together.

"I cannot believe as they do," he says. "And they need purity of belief."

"I don't understand," I say.

He sighs and pushes a long strand of hair away from his face. "He said we were raised to be ashamed of who we are. I still am. I cringe when they go through the rituals."

"What do you believe is happening at Mount Rushmore?" I keep my voice quiet, so as not to break this, the first thread of confidence he has ever shown in me.

"I'm like you," he says. His hands clutch the top of the wheel, knuckles white. "I don't care what is happening, as long as it provides emotion for my art."

***

WE LEAVE THE NEXT MORNING on a six a.m. flight. The plane is nearly empty. The reporters and tourists remain, since no one has any answers yet. The first suspect has been released, and another brought into custody. Specialists in every area from virtual reality to sculpture have flooded the site. Experts on Native Americans posit everything from a bombing to Coyote paying one last, great trick.

I have written everything but this, the final section. My hands shook last night as I typed in my conversation with Kenny. I am paid to observe, paid to learn, paid to be detached—but he is right. So few stories tug my own heartstrings. I won't let this one. I refuse to believe in miracles. I too want to see the experts prove that some odd technology has caused the change in the mountainside.

Yet as I lean back and try to imagine what that moment will feel like—the moment when I learn that some clever person with a hidden camera has caused the entire mess—I feel a sinking in my stomach. I want to believe in the miracle, and since I cannot, I want to have the chance to believe. I don't want anyone to take that small thing away from me.

Yet the old man's words do not fill me with comfort either. For the future he sees, the future he hopes for, has no place for me or my kind in it. Whatever has happened to the natives has happened to them, and not to me. Please God, never to me.

The sunlight has a sharp, early morning clarity. As the plane lifts off, its shadow moves like a hawk over the earth. My gaze follows the shadow, watching it move over buildings and then over the hills. As we pull up into the cloud, I gasp.

For below me, the hills have transformed into a reclining woman, her head tilted back, her knees bent, her breasts firm and high. She watches us until we disappear.

Until we leave the center of the world.

About the Author

INTERNATIONAL BESTSELLING WRITER Kristine Kathryn Rusch has published fiction in every genre. She has been nominated for three Edgar Awards, two Shamus Awards, and an Anthony Award. She has won the *Ellery Queen* Reader's Choice Award twice. She has also published award-winning mystery novels under the name Kris Nelscott. For more about her work, go to kristinekathrynrusch.com.

Also by
Kristine Kathryn Rusch

The Retrieval Artist Series:

The Disappeared
Extremes
Consequences
Buried Deep
Paloma
Recovery Man
Duplicate Effort
Anniversary Day
Blowback

The Smokey Dalton Series (as Kris Nelscott):

A Dangerous Road
Smoke-Filled Rooms
Thin Walls
Stone Cribs
War at Home
Days of Rage
Street Justice (March 2014)